"Look," she told him, "this doesn't have anything to do with my, er, my..."

"Virginity?" he asked.

Kimberly gulped in a breath of air before saying, "Not the way you're thinking. What I mean is..."

"Yes?" Cort grinned.

Suddenly tongue-tied, she wanted to scream. Oh, for heaven's sake. She was going to say it, or die trying. Raising her chin as high as it would go, Kimberly said, "What I'm trying to tell you is this. That night when you...when I...when we..."

"Yes?"

A hundred words zinged through her mind. But when she opened her mouth to speak, she managed to breathe only two of them.

"I'm pregnant."

Dear Reader,

What happens when six brides and six grooms wed for *convenient* reasons? Well… In Donna Clayton's *Daddy Down the Aisle*, a confirmed bachelor becomes a FABULOUS FATHER—with the love of an adorable toddler…and his beautiful bride.

One night of passion leaves a (usually) prim woman expecting a BUNDLE OF JOY! In Sandra Steffen's *For Better, For Baby*, the mom-to-be marries the dad-to-be—and now they have nine months to fall in love….

From secretarial pool to wife of the handsome boss! Well, for a while. In Alaina Hawthorne's *Make-Believe Bride*, she hopes to be his Mrs. Forever—after all, that's how long she's loved him!

What's a rancher to do when his ex-wife turns up on his doorstep with amnesia and a big, juicy kiss? In Val Whisenand's *Temporary Husband*, he simply "forgets" to remind her that they're divorced….

Disguised as lovey-dovey newlyweds on a honeymoon at the Triple Fork Ranch, not-so-loving police partners uncover their own wedded bliss in Laura Anthony's *Undercover Honeymoon*….

In debut author Cathy Forsythe's *The Marriage Contract*, a sexy cowboy proposes a marriage of convenience, but when his bride discovers the real reason he said "I do"—watch out!

I hope you enjoy all six of our wonderful CONVENIENTLY WED titles this month—and all of the Silhouette Romance novels to come!

Regards,

Melissa Senate
Senior Editor

Please address questions and book requests to:
Silhouette Reader Service
U.S.: 3010 Walden Ave., P.O. Box 1325, Buffalo, NY 14269
Canadian: P.O. Box 609, Fort Erie, Ont. L2A 5X3

FOR BETTER, FOR BABY

Sandra Steffen

Conveniently Wed

Silhouette® ROMANCE™
Published by Silhouette Books
America's Publisher of Contemporary Romance

If you purchased this book without a cover you should be aware that this book is stolen property. It was reported as "unsold and destroyed" to the publisher, and neither the author nor the publisher has received any payment for this "stripped book."

For my husband, Ernie,
the most charming, funny, sexy
and exasperating man I know.

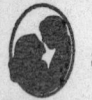

SILHOUETTE BOOKS

ISBN 0-373-19163-4

FOR BETTER, FOR BABY

Copyright © 1996 by Sandra E. Steffen

All rights reserved. Except for use in any review, the reproduction or utilization of this work in whole or in part in any form by any electronic, mechanical or other means, now known or hereafter invented, including xerography, photocopying and recording, or in any information storage or retrieval system, is forbidden without the written permission of the editorial office, Silhouette Books, 300 East 42nd Street, New York, NY 10017 U.S.A.

All characters in this book have no existence outside the imagination of the author and have no relation whatsoever to anyone bearing the same name or names. They are not even distantly inspired by any individual known or unknown to the author, and all incidents are pure invention.

This edition published by arrangement with Harlequin Books S.A.

® and TM are trademarks of Harlequin Books S.A., used under license. Trademarks indicated with ® are registered in the United States Patent and Trademark Office, the Canadian Trade Marks Office and in other countries.

Printed in U.S.A.

Books by Sandra Steffen

Silhouette Romance

Child of Her Dreams #1005
*Bachelor Daddy #1028
*Bachelor at the Wedding #1045
*Expectant Bachelor #1056
Lullaby and Goodnight #1074
A Father for Always #1138
For Better, For Baby #1163

Silhouette Desire

Gift Wrapped Dad #972

*Wedding Wager

SANDRA STEFFEN

Creating memorable characters is one of Sandra's favorite aspects of writing. She's always been a romantic, and is thrilled to be able to spend her days doing what she loves—bringing her characters to life on her computer screen.

Sandra grew up in Michigan, the fourth of ten children, all of whom have taken the old adage "Go forth and multiply" quite literally. Add to this her husband, who is her real-life hero, their four school-age sons who keep their lives in constant motion, their gigantic cat, Percy, and her wonderful friends, in-laws and neighbors, and what do you get? Chaos, of course, but also a wonderful sense of belonging she wouldn't trade for the world.

THE EXPECTANT BRIDE SPEAKS:

I, Kimberly Wilson, agree to marry Cort Sutherland because of the baby. It has not been my intention to trap him into a loveless marriage. But if my husband-to-be insists we do the right thing and marry, I'm not about to argue. Because even though I have no idea how we'll ever get along during the days, I'm certain we'll enjoy our wedding night—and all the nights to follow.

THE SURPRISED GROOM RESPONDS:

I, Cort Sutherland, am okay with my impending marriage to Kimberly Wilson. She is, after all, going to be the mother of my child. My child! I can't believe I'm going to be somebody's daddy, let alone somebody's husband. But Kimberly's going to be busy with the baby—she won't have time to disrupt my carefree schedule. And after all, how tough could marriage be?

Chapter One

"Aunt Kimberly, it's just what I've always wanted!"

Kimberly Wilson loved the way her nephew's sturdy arms wound around her neck for a quick hug as he thanked her for his new official major league baseball bat. Laughing along with everyone else, she looked on as the child sank back to his knees and tore into another package with all the glee of the well-adjusted seven-year-old boy he was.

She loved her only nephew more than she thought possible, but being with Tommy on his birthday wasn't the only reason she'd flown out from Boston today. A noise in the next room drew her attention away from the paper and ribbons flying through the air. She peeked around her sister and saw the outer door swing open. Moments later, the *other* reason she came back to this remote ranch in Nebraska walked into the room.

Outwardly, she didn't move, but inside, her heart sped up and her thoughts spun. She'd almost had herself convinced that Cort Sutherland couldn't possibly be as lean and rugged as she remembered. He *had* been undeniably attractive in the suit and tie he'd worn as best man in his brother's wedding more than two months ago. But today, he was even taller in his scuffed cowboy boots, and his faded jeans and jacket looked every bit as good on him as the most expensive suit ever could.

"You're late!" Evelyn Sutherland told her son in a scolding tone of voice mothers reserved for their children no matter how old they were.

Few things escaped Tommy's notice, and his uncle's arrival was no exception. He jumped to his feet and twirled around, shouting, "Uncle Cort, where's my present?"

Hidden as she was from Cort's view, Kimberly noticed the excited glances her sister's new family all shared as they gathered around Tommy. Something was going on, and it appeared as though she and Tommy were the only two people in the room who didn't know what it was.

"Did you get him unloaded?" Will asked quietly.

"Did you get who unloaded?" Tommy cut in.

"Let's go have your birthday cake," Krista called.

"But I want to see what Uncle Cort unloaded."

"Come on," Krista whispered close to Kimberly's ear. "If we don't get that little boy into the kitchen now, we never will."

With nerves climbing up and down her spine, Kimberly rose to her feet and fell into step behind her sister. This was the moment she'd been waiting for. Now that it was almost here, she wasn't sure she was ready.

"Cort, you remember my sister, Kimberly, don't you?" Krista asked, stepping to one side.

Cort swung around, his eyes meeting hers. For an interminable span of time, he seemed as frozen to the spot as Kimberly was. The rim of his brown cowboy hat cast part of his face in shadow, but it couldn't hide his reaction to seeing her again. His blue eyes widened, his chin lowered and his lips parted in surprise.

Disappointment sent a sourness to her already churning stomach. She'd known that it would be too much to expect that he'd be thrilled to see her again, but she'd hoped he'd at least be pleased. She hadn't counted on his cool reserve.

Aware of all the people watching, she did her best not to let the instant hurt show and quietly said, "Hello, Cort."

Cort Sutherland tried to tell himself that the reason the faces of people he'd known all his life had blurred was because he'd turned his head too fast. Strangely, Kimberly Wilson's features remained in perfect focus. She was wearing a pale blue pantsuit that looked soft and feminine and far removed from the clothes women in these parts wore. Her blond hair was parted on one side, waving freely to her shoulders, and her skin looked as pale and as flawless as it had the first time he saw her.

He might have been able to come up with the right thing to say if he'd known she was coming. As it was, all he could do was nod.

"Uncle Cort, what did you bring me? Huh? What is it?"

He heard Tommy's question, but he couldn't take his eyes off Kimberly. He didn't like the silence stretching between them. He liked feeling like a heel even less.

She lowered her eyes, and Cort was finally able to turn his attention to Tommy and say, "You heard your mother, partner. Cake and ice cream first. Your birthday present second."

"Aw, gee," Tommy said, shaking his head. "Come on, everybody. We might as well get this over with."

Kimberly was thankful for the noise and commotion taking place all around her. It gave her a moment to swallow her disappointment and square her shoulders. Trying to focus on Tommy, she followed the child into the kitchen, being careful to steer clear of Cort at the same time.

Once the Sutherlands had gathered around the table, chaos erupted once again. Krista and her mother-in-law laughed at something Tommy said. Cort was paying rapt attention to the conversation between his father and brother, seemingly oblivious to her presence. Tommy flitted from one adult to another, acting for all the world as if he'd been born to this family, though he and his mother had only become Sutherlands two months ago. Hurting in ways she should have been accustomed to by now, Kimberly wondered if she'd ever truly belong anywhere.

While Will and Krista passed out plates, she reached into the freezer for the carton of ice cream, more confused than she'd ever been. That was saying a lot, because she'd been confused most of her life. As a child prodigy, she'd been forced to attend special schools, to take tests, to perform and to achieve. Even as an adult, her "gift" had ruled her existence. It had always amazed her that others found her abilities so fascinating. Just once, she'd like someone to be fascinated by *who* she was, instead of *what* she was.

Conversation went on all around her, but Kimberly's thoughts spun like dust on a prairie whirlwind. They took her back to the day Will and Krista had been married two and a half months ago. She could almost see the glow of candlelight and hear the February wind that had whistled through the church that evening. More than anything, she remembered the promise she'd made to herself to take charge of her own life and find the kind of happiness she'd always longed for.

It had seemed predestined that the man standing opposite her had drawn her gaze and her longings as no one else ever had, but what was even more amazing was the fact that he'd seemed drawn to her in return. She'd never known a man like Cort Sutherland, a man who worked from sunup to sundown, as much a part of his ranch as the soil and fence posts themselves, a man whose eyes darkened each time they rested on her. For the first time in her life, she'd felt feminine and graceful, winsome and beautiful. For the first time in her life she'd felt like a woman, normal in every way.

She hadn't wanted to leave the next day, but knew there were things she had to do in Boston. So she'd boarded the plane, taking her fledgling determination with her. Being a genius had its rewards. One of them was a healthy bank account, which allowed her the freedom to give notice as a systems analyst for a prestigious corporation in downtown Boston. Without work to fill her days, she'd enrolled in an art class, took long walks and pondered her future. And she wondered if her name ever crept into Cort Sutherland's mind.

The slightly out-of-tune voices singing "Happy Birthday" drew her from her daydream. When the song ended, Krista smoothed down a stubborn lock of hair on the top of Tommy's head and quietly said, "Now you can make a wish and blow out your candles."

Tommy smiled impishly and said, "My wishes always come true."

"Oh, they do, do they?" his new grandpa asked.

"Sure they do," Tommy replied. "I wished for a puppy, and I got Blue. I wished for a daddy, and I got the best one in the world. Now I want a baby brother who looks just like me."

Kimberly laughed in spite of herself. Like his three aunts, Tommy's intellect bordered on genius. Unlike them, he believed with all his heart in wishes and dreams come true.

Leaning closer to Tommy, Krista said, "Your dad and I would like to have a baby, too, kiddo, but we can't guarantee that it'll be a boy or that it'll have dark hair and eyes like you. Your little brother or sister could be blond and blue-eyed like Aunt Kimberly."

"Fair of face and full of grace?" Tommy asked.

Kimberly's smile suddenly felt tight and unnatural. She closed her eyes, wondering if Cort was thinking that she wasn't full of grace anymore. She forced her eyes open again and found him watching her closely.

Without his hat, his dark brown hair showed the paths his fingers had taken when they'd raked it straight off his forehead. Lines of concentration formed between his eyebrows. Something flickered far back in his eyes, and he smiled.

Kimberly's breath caught just below the hollow in her throat, and a sound too soft to be heard by anyone else echoed deep inside. He accepted the plate his brother was shoving into his hands, but even after he'd turned his attention back to the party, his lips continued to bear a faint smile.

More confused than ever, Kimberly handed the ice cream to Krista and sank into a nearby chair.

The April sun hovered at the very edge of the horizon, casting swirls of pink and lavender into the western sky. Kimberly had been watching the colors change for almost an hour, no closer to reaching a decision about her future than she'd been a month ago.

Were other thirty-year-old women such fools? Or was she in a class all by herself? Everything had seemed so easy, so cut-and-dried and promising, all those weeks ago when she'd first made her vow to find happiness. Now, the future seemed vague and shadowy.

She'd been so sure she'd know what to do if she just saw Cort again. She'd half hoped that what she felt for him before had more to do with romantic notions than real feelings. What she was experiencing now was so real it scared her. She'd been disappointed at his initial reaction to seeing her again, but the smile he'd given her in the kitchen had turned her heart to feather down.

What did that smile mean? Was it possible that he cared about her? What should she do? What would be best? The same thoughts played through her mind over and over, ceaseless, inner questions that had no answers.

A horse's whinny carried to her ears on the late-evening breeze, followed by Tommy's awe-filled laughter. Everyone had finished their cake and ice cream an hour and a half ago. With his special, insuppressible excitement, Tommy had herded them all through the door, intent upon discovering what his father and uncle had up their sleeves. Barely out the back door, he'd let out a whoop that would have made any cowboy proud.

"A horse! Is he mine?"

"He's yours all right, son," Will had said.

They'd all exclaimed over the gelding, but only Blue, Tommy's half-grown puppy, could match his exuberance. Joe and Evelyn Sutherland had left half an hour ago, honking their horn on their way out of the driveway. Cort's departure fifteen minutes later had been much quieter and a lot more confusing.

The spring evening was turning cooler with the setting of the sun, but Tommy wasn't ready to leave his new horse and come inside. He giggled out loud as Will showed him how to hold his hand so the bay could nuzzle grass from his palm. "Oh, Daddy," he said, "Socks is just what I've always wanted."

There was something about the way Tommy said *Daddy* that sent tears to Kimberly's eyes. Although Will had started adoption proceedings immediately after his marriage to Krista, the process was far from complete. Evidently, Tommy didn't care about legalities. For all veritable intents and purposes, Will Sutherland was already his father in every way that mattered.

"They're really something, aren't they?" Krista asked, taking a sip of coffee from one of the mugs in her hand before lowering to the step next to her.

Kimberly accepted the coffee and inhaled the aroma. But she didn't take a sip. Her eyes were on the little boy on the other side of the driveway. Will started to lead the bay away, but Tommy nudged his way in between Will and the horse as if it was the most natural thing in the world.

"I've never seen Tommy so happy," Kimberly said when they disappeared around the side of the barn.

"Neither have I," Krista said softly.

"Will, either, for that matter."

"Mmm," Krista answered around a sip of coffee. "Tommy's happy. Will's happy. I'm happy. Now what are we going to do about you?"

Kimberly turned her head and found her only brown-eyed sister watching her intently. "What do you mean?" she asked quietly.

Krista was also the only Wilson sister whose IQ didn't register in the genius range, yet she'd always had the innate ability to see into the heart of the people she loved. She was more sure of herself, and always seemed to know the right thing to do. Kimberly would gladly choose a lower IQ in exchange for those traits.

"I know you have something on your mind, and I thought you might want to talk about it."

"I'm fine, Krista. Really."

"I'm glad. But you're pale, and you've barely said more than ten words since you arrived this morning."

Kimberly shrugged, suddenly very tired. She'd always yearned for the kind of closeness she and Krista were beginning to share, but the memory of Cort's smile and of the way he'd been with Tommy was still too fresh in her mind to talk about. She'd come to Nebraska today because she just *had* to see Cort again, to look into his eyes and try to determine if he had any feelings for her whatsoever.

She'd done every one of those things. And she was still sitting here attempting to make up her mind. In a flash of revelation, she knew what she had to do. Trying for a light tone of voice, she said, "There was a lot of air turbulence in the flight out here this morning. I probably have jet lag."

"Maybe you should lie down."

"Actually, I was thinking about taking a drive."

"By yourself?" Krista asked.

"If you wouldn't mind."

Without another word, Krista was on her feet. Taking the unused cup of coffee from Kimberly's hand, she strode into the house. She returned seconds later and dropped a set of keys into Kimberly's palm, saying, "Take a left out of the driveway and go two miles, then turn right onto Schavey Road. It's three miles on the left."

"What is?" Kimberly asked.

"Cort's place. What else?"

With a wink and a smile, Krista skipped down the steps and made her way across the yard toward the barn and her husband and son. Kimberly found her feet more slowly. Since there was no sense wondering how Krista could have known, Kimberly took a deep breath for courage and set off to do what she had to do.

* * *

Cort pushed through the outer door and sank into the painted metal chair on his front porch. He leaned back and propped his booted feet on the railing, just like he had a hundred times before.

Ahh. That was better. He'd just sit out here and watch the sun go down over Sutherland property.

He hadn't been able to make head or tail of the ledgers and receipts spread out on the kitchen table, and he knew why. That didn't mean he was going to allow the reason to barge into his thoughts again. Uh-uh, no way, absolutely not. He'd just relax out here in the April night and plan his week. There was certainly plenty to think about. It was spring, the busiest time of the year, if you didn't count summer, winter or fall.

The herd had gotten rangy like they always did over the winter. He and Will and a few of the hired hands had rounded up the strays, but there were still a thousand things to do. Fences needed mending, horses needed to be shod, calves would be born, and cattle needed to be branded, fed and duly fattened. One of the hired hands had walked off the job yesterday, which was going to leave them shorthanded. But they'd get by, just like they always did.

Cort scooched deeper into the chair, his leather boots creaking slightly as he crossed one ankle over the other. Nights tended to get cool this time of the year, but pretty soon it would be summer, and cool breezes would be distant memories, especially out on the range.

That's it. Just keep thinking about the ranch.

Morris Blakely was going to deliver that new bull tomorrow. That meant they'd have to double-check the gates and fences. The grass on the range east of the creek was getting dangerously short. Since he couldn't risk the wind cutting blowouts into the hills, they'd have to move those cattle to another grazing place farther west. Tomorrow, he'd talk to Mo and Frank and Pokey about it. While he was at it, he'd ask if any of them knew of a good cowhand who was looking for work.

Ah, yes, thinking about the ranch was working its magic. He was focused, calmer, more in charge.

In the west, the sun was all but gone for another day, taking the glorious colors of sunset with it, leaving only the faintest traces of blue behind. Staring past his boots, Cort's breathing deepened. There wasn't another color on earth as changeable as blue. It could be as dark and mysterious as midnight or as soft and innocent as dawn.

Like Kimberly's eyes.

His feet hit the floor with a thud, the chair creaking in his haste to push out of it. Gritting his teeth, he ordered the color blue from his thoughts.

Think about white. White was a safe color. Snow was white. Cold, wet snow. The fence posts around the corral were white, too. Yes, white was a good color, a soothing color, like porches or clouds or rich cream.

Or Kimberly's soft, supple skin.

His eyes closed as he remembered how the hollow at the base of her throat had felt beneath his lips. Desire inched through his veins, lower, thicker, stronger.

Forget about her, he said to himself. Forget about the way her waist had fit his hands, and the way his heart had lurched each time she'd sighed. Forget about the shy smile she'd given him moments before he'd kissed her that night after Will and Krista's wedding, and how, much later, she'd been anything but shy.

Oh, for crying out loud.

He shoved his hands to his hips, giving up any pretense he might have had of keeping one blue-eyed genius out of his thoughts. Turning toward the door, he decided to give the ledgers another try.

The sound of an approaching car stilled his forward motion. His eyes narrowed, and his hands fell to his sides. It looked like his sister-in-law's car. That was strange. What in the world would Krista be doing here now?

As the car pulled into the driveway, his thoughts slowed. The engine was cut; the door was pushed open. When the porch light spilled over pale blond hair instead of dark brown, his thoughts seemed to stop completely, and something else took control of his body. Maybe this was an aberration. Maybe it was a mirage. Or maybe every fantasy he'd had these past few months was coming to life before his very eyes.

"I was hoping you'd still be up," Kimberly called, taking a tentative step toward him.

He recognized the wavering shyness in her voice. It did nothing to chase away the need pooling low in his body.

"I'm not bothering you, am I?" she asked.

She was bothering him all right, in the most incredible of ways. Leaning a hip against the railing, he crossed his arms and said, "I don't mind."

"Really?"

He nodded, and she took another few steps toward the porch.

He got so caught up in watching her walk toward him he almost forgot his manners. Coming to his senses, he finally said, "Are you out for an evening drive?"

She stopped, one foot on the first step, the other on the grass below. "Not exactly," she said, her voice throaty, her eyes huge in her pale face. "Krista gave me directions. Of course, she doesn't know I've been here before."

Cort nodded, understanding. He hadn't told anyone of her one and only other visit to his place, either.

She hemmed and hawed for a moment, then said, "There's something I have to do. Something I have to talk to you about."

Suddenly, all the nights he'd lain awake with nothing but his memories, the sheets a tangled heap at his feet, came together in a moment of raw need. He reached for her hands, bodily drawing her up to him.

"There's something I have to do, too," he declared, his voice a husky rasp in the cool, still night.

Cort's heart pounded an erratic rhythm as he lowered his face to hers. Her eyes, those blue, blue eyes, opened wide, then lowered dreamily. If blue had a texture, it would be velvet; if it had a sound, it would be that of the slowly drawn breath she took through lips shaped by a quiet "Oh."

He moved his mouth over hers, her surprise turning into a sultry sigh that sent blood pulsing through his body. This was no aberration, no mirage. It was passion, and it was as real as the woman in his arms.

Kimberly was certain the boards beneath her feet were tilting. Cort's kisses were slow and drugging, his mouth moving over hers hungrily, his hands sliding around her back, fitting her closer, tighter, to his body. The warmth of his breath on her cheek sent the pit of her stomach into a wild swirl. His lips were intimate, demanding a response to equal his. He'd kissed her before, but tonight he seemed ravenous, like a man a long time denied.

Months ago she'd been shocked at her eager response to the touch of his lips on hers, but not anymore. Now, she reveled in the feelings coursing through her, in the sounds of his breathing, and hers, in the strength of the arms around her, and the hard ridge of him pressing against the exact place she'd rested her palm so many times this past month.

A thought shimmered in the very back of her mind, but with her nerve endings dancing every place Cort touched, it was difficult to focus on what it was. She'd come here to tell him something. She wondered what it was.

The whisker stubble on his chin rasped against her cheek, his chest expanding with every breath he took. He was incredible, virile in every way, the muscles in his back and thighs well-defined. She was amazed at how well she remembered, and was in awe of how wonderful it felt to be back in his arms.

His mouth left hers on a gasp for air, only to press a kiss into the hollow below her ear. Kimberly tipped her head to one side, her hands gliding over his shoulders, molding him closer to her, his hardness pushing against her soft belly.

There it was again, a thought trying to make its way through the thick haze of passion. His lips trailed moist, hot kisses over her jaw, along her cheekbone, drawing a response from deep inside her. Before that response carried her away again, she turned her head, his lips skimming her cheek instead of her mouth. Her eyes fluttered open. Her thoughts stilled, and so did her hands.

"Cort, we have to stop."

"We're just getting started."

He'd spoken on a whisper, his lips brushing her sensitive skin with every word. Her knees almost buckled, and her concentration nearly slipped away all over again. Some thread of rationality must have remained, because her hands found their way to his chest, resolve finding its way through her mind and body.

"This isn't why I came here tonight," she whispered, levering herself away from him.

He loosened his hold, but didn't remove his hands completely. "I, for one, am glad you're here."

A smile might have found its way to her mouth if she hadn't reminded herself of the reason she'd come to Nebraska—more importantly, the reason she'd driven out here tonight. She couldn't lose sight of what she had to do, no matter how good his simple declaration made her feel.

Taking another deep breath for courage, she finally stepped out of his embrace and strode to the other end of the narrow porch. Gazing out into the darkness, she said, "There's something I have to tell you, Cort."

"You can actually think about talking after kissing me like that?"

He'd spoken with a cocky self-confidence that was the essence of the man himself. Although she wasn't facing him, she heard the smile in his voice. There was no stopping the softening sensation around her heart, but when his boots creaked slightly as he moved closer, she drew herself up to her full height and turned around to face him.

"I'm not sure where to begin."

"Does this have anything to do with the reason Krista was watching me so closely at Tommy's party earlier?" he asked.

She looked at him sharply, then shook her head. "If Krista was watching you closely, there must be another reason, because I haven't told anyone my secret."

"Neither have I, Kimberly. You have to know I never would."

She stared wordlessly at him, wondering how in the world he could have known about her secret. Beneath his heated look, realization dawned. She swallowed tightly and said, "I don't think we're talking about the same thing, Cort."

Walking ever closer, he said, "Aren't you talking about the night Will and Krista were married? And about what happened between us?"

"Look," she cut in, certain that if she didn't stop him there would be no blood left in her face whatsoever. She was doing this badly, and his reference to that night wasn't helping. "This doesn't have anything to do with my, er, my..."

"Virginity?" he asked, his voice dipping low.

She gulped in a breath of air before saying, "Not the way you're thinking. What I mean is..."

"Yes?"

"Look, I think we've gotten off track here. *That* isn't the secret I'm referring to."

"What exactly are you referring to?" he asked, his eyes narrowing more with every word.

Suddenly tongue-tied, she wanted to scream. Oh, for heaven's sake. She'd spent more hours in a classroom than even she could count. She was fluent in four languages, and could unravel the trickiest calculus equation without batting an eye. She had a photographic memory and could cite statistics as if it were second nature. Why hadn't she ever learned how to get to the point?

All right. This was it. She was going to say it, or die trying. Raising her chin as high as it would go, she said, "What I'm trying to tell you is this. That night when you... When I... When we..."

"Yes?"

A hundred words zinged through her mind. But when she opened her mouth to speak, she managed to breathe only two of them.

"I'm pregnant."

Chapter Two

Cort stared at Kimberly, far too dumbfounded to think, let alone speak. Somewhere in the distance, a cow lowed. The only other sound he heard was his own blood pounding into his head. Through the roaring din in his ears, he finally managed to whisper, "You're what?"

"I'm pregnant. I'm going to have a baby."

His mind flashed back to the night he'd spent with her. As her sister's maid of honor, Kimberly had been femininely graceful and beguilingly shy. As far as he was concerned, it had been one helluva potent combination. He doubted he'd ever forget how wild she'd become in his arms that night. The memory alone had kept him awake nearly every night since.

He raked his fingers through his hair, silently cursing himself and the heat pooling low in his body. This was hardly the time or the place.

With his misgivings increasing by the second, he bit out the first thing that came to mind. "I know what the hell it means, Kimberly. I thought you said it was safe."

He regretted the words the moment they were out. The color drained out of her face, which only made him feel worse. A lesser woman might have cowered, but not Kimberly. She raised her chin another notch and simply said, "I thought so, too."

A string of swear words whistled through his head. Taking a deep breath, he made sure they didn't get any farther. He didn't have to ask if the baby was his. Aside from the fact that she'd been a virgin their one and only night together, he instinctively knew she wouldn't be here unless the baby was his.

The baby. It was his turn to go pale.

She crossed her arms close to her body and glanced around, awarding him an opportunity to take a deep breath and study her more closely. Her hair glowed a pale yellow beneath the bulb of the porch light. Until tonight, he hadn't noticed the dark smudges beneath her eyes, but her skin looked as smooth and flawless as he remembered.

His gaze continued over her face, touching upon her pert nose and full lips, and down the creamy expanse of her neck where a small hollow was visible above the V of her pale blue top. Several inches lower, her chest rose and fell with every breath she took.

With desire pounding ever thicker in his body, he brought his gaze back to her face, and froze. Sometime during his perusal, she'd raised her eyes to his, and caught him looking.

The color was back in her cheeks. She neither apologized for it, nor tried to disguise it. She simply said, "You must have questions."

Questions? Of course he had questions. A million at least. Unfortunately, he couldn't think of a single one, at least not at this particular moment. All he could think about was what her nearness was doing to his senses, and how he wanted to unfasten those shiny blue buttons, then slowly push the fabric from her shoulders.

Obviously misinterpreting his silence for anxiety of another nature, she softened her voice to the tone he'd heard her use with Tommy and said, "Believe me, I know what a huge surprise this is. I've had an entire month to think about it, to adjust. You've only had a few minutes. You probably don't know what to think, let alone say."

Skirting around him, she headed for the steps. Pausing at the bottom, she added, "You're a decent man, and I felt you deserved to know, but don't worry, I don't expect anything from you."

Without another word, she strode to Krista's car and got in. He watched her drive away, the apprehension that had been flickering through him fast turning into a volcano on the verge of erupting. His feet were rooted to the floor, but his mind was racing.

She expected nothing from him? Nothing?

He saw the car fall into a pothole. It was already caked with dirt, which completely obliterated her taillights. Cort saw red just the same. His thoughts came in spurts, his breathing became ragged and his hands clenched into fists at his sides.

She thought she could just waltz over here and drop her little bomb, then waltz out again, expecting nothing from him?

Anger propelled him forward with incredible force. He shoved the metal chair out of his way so hard it slammed against the house with a loud bang. Frustration, so potent he could taste it, lengthened his stride. Even the slamming of the screen door behind him didn't slow his steps.

He paced through his sparsely furnished living room and on into the kitchen. There, he finally stopped. He stared at the ledgers and receipts spread out on the table, but his thoughts were on something else entirely.

Kimberly was going to have a baby.

No. She wasn't going to have just any baby. She was going to have *his* baby. And by God, whether she expected anything from him or not, she was going to get it.

Cort's old truck kicked up gravel as it rattled over the county road that led to Will's place. The low drone of the weather report played over the radio. He barely heard. He felt much calmer today, no matter what Pokey and Charlie said. Okay, maybe he had been a little short-tempered with his two best cowhands. But Pokey, whose memory wasn't what it used to be, would have forgotten it by suppertime, and Charlie was only nineteen and had the rest of his life to get over it.

Loosening the death grip he had on the steering wheel, Cort reminded himself of the iron will he'd imposed upon himself somewhere around three in the morning. Be calm. Be rational. Be nice. Yes, he was definitely handling the situation a lot better this morning.

He'd gone over every single word Kimberly had said last night, every subtle nuance of her expression. The woman had kissed him senseless, but in the end, she'd looked him in the eye and told him the truth. In the process, she'd also told him that she thought he was a decent man. Under the circumstances, she could have said a lot worse. But she was right. As a Sutherland, he came from a long line of decent men and women who worked hard at living, and at doing the right thing. Now all he had to do was calmly and rationally explain that to Kimberly.

Gravel churned beneath his tires as he downshifted and braked. By the time he'd pulled to a stop behind the car Kimberly had driven last night, Tommy came out of the house toting a backpack and an expression far too knowing for his years.

"I knew it," he sputtered. "Something's going on, and I'm going to miss it."

"What do you mean?"

"Well, Mommy and Aunt Kimberly are whispering, and now you've shown up. And rats, here comes the bus."

Cort half wished Pokey and Charlie could have heard his deep chuckle. Ruffling Tommy's hair, he said, "Going to school will be good for you. It'll make you smart."

"I'm already smart."

The kid had a point, and Cort couldn't help grinning as he watched Tommy run to the end of the driveway where the bus pulled to a stop. Still smiling, Cort strode into his brother's kitchen where three pairs of eyes darted to his. Suddenly, his grin felt out of place.

"Good morning!" Krista called, her brown eyes as knowing as Tommy's had been.

"Will, Krista," he said curtly, quickly removing his hat. "Kimberly," he added, slower, quieter, throatier.

Will and Krista exchanged a look, picked up their mugs of coffee, then made noises about drinking it in the other room. They were about as subtle as a hailstorm, but Cort didn't care. He had something to say to Kimberly, and he preferred to do it in private.

His brother and sister-in-law left, and he and Kimberly were alone in the sunny kitchen. All ready to begin, he turned to look at her. Just like that, all his carefully rehearsed words stuck in his throat. Her hair was slightly disheveled, and he was certain there was more color in her cheeks this morning. She looked all rosy and rested, and, damn, she was beautiful.

She slipped her hands into the pockets of her jade green robe and cast him a sidelong glance. "Krista said you'd show up here this morning. I guess I didn't realize she meant *this* early." Shrugging a little sheepishly, she added, "I'm afraid I haven't had time to get dressed."

There it was again, that low hum making its way through his body. It happened every time she looked at him, her expression beguilingly shy, her movements infinitely feminine. Struggling to hold on to his composure, he strode closer. Keeping his voice low, he asked, "Then Krista and Will know about the baby?"

She nodded. "I told Krista. She told Will. And Tommy's fit to be tied because he isn't in on the secret." Turning sharply, she said, "I hope you don't mind. I mean, Will is your brother, and you probably would have liked to tell him yourself."

"No, no, I hadn't really thought about it, but this is fine."

He hesitated, once again at a loss for words. Suddenly, he wondered if maybe he should have done a little more experimenting with one-night stands and casual sex. At least then he might have known how to handle mornings after. Problem was, he'd never much cared for one-night stands, and he'd never believed there was anything casual about sex. The night he'd spent with Kimberly had pretty much proved that theory.

She'd slipped out of his bed in the wee hours of the morning, and he hadn't seen her again until yesterday. Evidently, mornings after had to be dealt with sooner or later. He wished to high heaven he would have handled it as soon as it had happened. If he had, he might not have felt as if he were walking through a mine field today.

She glanced up when he neared, her hair falling to the front of her shoulder. He automatically reached for the long tendrils, effortlessly smoothing them back again. Her gaze met his, held, then fell away again. Tipping her head toward a glass carafe, she said, "Would you like a cup of coffee?"

With a mild shake of his head, he said, "I never acquired a taste for it, but you go ahead."

Placing one hand just below her ribs, she said, "I positively love it, but I'm afraid it doesn't love me, at least not lately. These past few mornings I've been munching on saltines for breakfast."

Her words brought him to his senses like a splash of cold water. She was talking about morning sickness. She was pregnant. That was why he was here.

"Are you all right? I mean, maybe you should sit down," he said.

Spinning away from him, she said, "I'm fine. Krista tells me I'll very likely live to tell about it. Now, I suppose you've come to ask a few questions. Let me start by assuring you that I intend to take very good care of myself and of the baby. I've already seen a doctor in Boston. According to the charts, the baby should be born around the first..."

"Of November," Cort cut in. Noting her surprise, he said, "I didn't mean to interrupt, but I did the math around two this morning."

"Instead of sleeping?" she asked.

"I had a lot on my mind," he said, his gaze following her as she smoothed her hand along the counter, meandering around the U-shaped kitchen.

In a tone of voice that was amazingly clear and mellow, she said, "I know how you feel. I stayed awake the entire night when I first found out, too. Believe me, it'll get better. I went straight to bed after telling you last night and slept like a baby."

Once again, a sensuous heat thrummed through Cort's body. Her words shouldn't have been provocative, yet they called to mind the night he'd awakened her with a kiss, which had turned into a touch, which had led to another incredible bout of lovemaking. He wondered which time had made her pregnant, not that it really mattered. What mattered was that they were going to have a baby.

"I've been thinking," he said, continuing to watch her movements around the room. "The Logan County seat is in Stapleton. That's where we'll have to go to get the license. I'm sure a judge could perform the ceremony there, too."

Kimberly turned slowly and stared at him.

Cort surged on. "Unless you'd prefer to have Reverend Jones do it. You remember him, don't you? He's the preacher who married Will and Krista."

"Cort, what are you talking about?"

Something in the tone of her voice gave him pause. Her eyes were wide open, the silence between them stretching tight with tension. He took a step toward her, settling his hands to his hips. "I'm talking about the wedding. Our wedding."

A soft gasp escaped her parted lips. The next thing he knew, she clamped her mouth shut, squared her shoulders and raised her chin in a way that could only mean trouble.

"Who said anything about getting married?" she asked, her voice cracking on the last word.

"I did. Why are you getting so worked up?"

"Worked up?" she asked incredulously. "You mention a wedding and I'm supposed to jump at the chance? Is that what you expect?"

He didn't like the accusation in her voice, and felt a muscle begin to work in his jaw. Irritation chafed like hay down the back of his shirt. He squared off opposite her and declared, "I'll tell you what I expect, dammit. I expect you to do the right thing. You have to marry me."

Her eyes literally glowed with a stubbornness he hadn't known she possessed. She set her shoulders and crossed her arms and said, "I have to do no such thing, Cort Sutherland."

The cold edge of irony sounded even more ominous in her carefully controlled voice. For some reason, her restraint made him all the more frustrated. "What are you saying?" he asked, grinding the words between his clenched teeth.

"I'm saying I didn't come to Nebraska to get married."

"Then what the hell are you doing here?"

Kimberly's breath caught in her throat. She felt herself shrinking from the anger in Cort's eyes, and turned away to keep him from seeing. Doing everything in her power to hide the sense of inadequacy that had a way of taking root in her mind and body, she held perfectly still. Aware of Cort's eyes on her back, she said, "I told you why I came last night. I didn't become pregnant on purpose, Cort, but I want this baby, and I *am* trying to do the right thing."

"Then marry me, dammit."

She shook her head one time, but she didn't look over her shoulder. For interminable seconds, the room was utterly still. Just when the tension and silence seemed unbearable, she heard the rustle of Cort's jeans and the creak of his boots behind her. The next sound she heard was the slamming of the back door.

Kimberly didn't know why she strode to the window, but once she was there, she couldn't look away. Cort's body language spoke volumes as he made his way toward his dusty old truck. Even angry, he had that easy grace and loose-jointed swagger people automatically associated with a cowboy. He plunked his hat on his head as if it was second nature, the early-morning sunshine making the rim appear lighter than the rest. She would have bet her last degree that the well-worn look of his jeans came from use, not chemicals. And his boots looked as if they'd walked more than a hundred miles.

He opened his truck door and climbed inside in one easy movement, his jeans molding tight to his backside and thighs. Her eyes fluttered down, then back up again, a similar sensation taking place low in her belly.

She wasn't well.

She'd responded to him physically the first time she saw him at Krista and Will's wedding. Today, she felt an even deeper tug on her insides. She folded her arms close to her heart, wishing they were Cort's instead.

She definitely wasn't well.

Kimberly watched him drive away, his tires kicking up stones, her thoughts kicking up confusion at every turn. Cort Sutherland was exactly the kind of man she thought she'd never find. Her attraction to him had been immediate and complete, his cocky self-confidence and boyish charm wreaking havoc with her senses. There was just something about the way he looked at her, something in the tone of his voice, in the touch of his hand, that had had her throwing caution to the wind. It had been completely out of character for her, but she wasn't sorry for the one night she'd spent in his arms. Maybe she'd gotten caught up in the romance of Krista's wedding, or maybe she'd gotten caught up in the warmth in Cort's eyes. After all, he was quite a man. Unfortunately, she had very little knowledge of the male half of the species.

Even though she could barely remember her father, she missed him now. He'd died when she and her sisters had all been very young. She'd grown up in a house of females, had attended special schools where she'd had little contact with *normal* men. Consequently, Kimberly knew very little about them, and understood them even less.

She cinched the sash of her long robe tighter about her waist, then folded her arms close to her heart, more than a little dismayed at what she'd just done. She'd turned down her first and only marriage proposal. Maybe she wasn't so brilliant, after all.

She'd had a sneaking suspicion that she was in love with Cort all those weeks ago. Now, her suspicions had been confirmed. She was in love with the father of her child. Then why hadn't she accepted his proposal?

In retrospect, she knew she shouldn't have been surprised that he'd offered to marry her. Demanded was more like it, she thought to herself with a wry twist of her lips. She'd instinctively known he was a decent, honorable man. He probably thought it had been a pretty good offer for a girl like her. Maybe he was right.

Three months ago, she might have accepted. But that was before she'd made that vow to herself to find real happiness. Although she didn't know what she was going to do about everything happening in her life, she knew she was going to fight to keep her promise. She was in love, truly in love, for the first time in her life. But she wouldn't marry a man who didn't love her in return.

Cort threw his leg over the saddle and slid to the ground. In no mood to wait for Will to do the same, he led his horse toward the corral and began inspecting the gate. The new bull snorted from a fenced-in area twenty-five feet away. It was all Cort could do not to answer with a snort of his own.

Morris Blakely had delivered the bull a couple of hours ago. The Brahman was huge and as ornery as they came. Although Cort respected the bull's sheer power and strength, he was pretty sure they could go head-to-head when it came to belligerence.

But then, so could Kimberly.

He'd gone back over to Will and Krista's to talk to her last night, certain that, given time, he'd be able to make her see reason. It hadn't taken him long to realize that there was no reasoning with that woman.

He'd been straightforward about his wishes, saying he wanted to give the baby his name. She'd promised to think about it. Okay, he'd thought. So far so good. Patiently, he'd told her that babies needed two parents. She'd said this baby would have two. Remaining calm, he said that wasn't what he meant. Kids needed parents who were married. She'd cited statistics and percentages about divorce rates and single-parent homes. Feeling his blood pressure rise, he'd asked her to marry him again. Again, she'd refused.

He'd never known anyone who made it look so easy to send his patience right through the roof. He'd managed to hold on to his temper while he was in her presence, but the other people in his life hadn't been so lucky. By now, everyone except Will was doing everything in their power to steer clear of him.

He slammed his shoulder against the gate, checking for loose boards. By the time he'd gone down on his haunches to check the bottom, Will's shadow had fallen across him.

"At this rate, you're going to have one helluva bruise tomorrow," Will said levelly.

"It wouldn't be the first time."

Cort hadn't intended to glance up at his brother. Once he did, he wished he wouldn't have. Eyes nearly the same color as his own were staring directly at him. Maybe he was overly sensitive this morning, but he was getting sick and darned tired of the way people around here kept looking at him.

"Know what I think?" Will asked.

"Oh, for crying out loud, not you, too. It seems that everyone and their brother wants to tell me what they think. Mom and Dad haven't stopped talking in hushed tones since I told them the news yesterday. Mo, Charlie and Frank all put in their two cents' worth first thing this morning. I guess I shouldn't have been surprised when Pokey, who's been a bachelor for most of this century, felt obligated to take me aside and offer me the wisdom of his years. But I never expected to hear it from you, Will. I'll tell you what I told everyone else. When I want advice, I'll ask for it, all right?"

Cort scowled and stood, fully expecting a good tongue-lashing from his only brother. So be it. He swiped his hands on his hips and cast Will a sidelong glance. Strangely, Will didn't look the least bit upset. He slapped the dirt from his gray cowboy hat and placed it on his head. Gazing at something far away, he said, "I wasn't referring to Kimberly with my last question. I was just going to tell you that I think it's safe to move the bull to this pen."

Will turned then, and with a limp that was barely discernable anymore, he strode to his horse and mounted. Feeling lower than a snake's belly, Cort squinted against the bright morning sun and watched him go. The bull snorted from the next pen. This time, Cort answered with a derisive snort of his own.

"All right," Cort declared, striding through the doorway and on into the barn where Will was working. "I'm sorry I spouted off earlier. I know it was uncalled for. Now I'm asking. What the hell am I going to do?"

"I don't know, Cort."

"What do you mean you don't know? Bachelors have been giving me advice at every turn. You've been married for more than two months. You must have gleaned an insight or two that would help me decide what to do."

Dust twinkled through the air on the slanted beams of sunlight streaming in through the window directly behind Will. Paying Cort and the sunlight equal amounts of attention—none—he loosened the last strap on the saddle and lifted it off. Cort knew better than to say anything else. When Will was ready, he'd talk. He only hoped to hell it would be soon.

The saddle creaked, and Will made a groaning sound as he heaved it onto the rack, and finally asked, "What do you want to do?"

Cort took a long step closer. "I want to marry that woman, that's what I want to do."

"And?"

"And she refuses."

"What are you going to do about it?" Will asked, removing the striped blanket from his horse's back.

"What can I do about it?" Cort said, his eyes narrowing.

"I guess that depends on you. And on Kimberly. If she's anything like her sister, she's as stubborn as she is tall. But if she's anything like Krista, she's also warm and gentle and pretty darned amazing. Tell me, Cort, just how well do you know Kimberly?"

For a moment, Cort thought he understood how a pitcher must have felt when Will Sutherland had been up to bat. Of course, everyone in the baseball industry had called him Billy-the-Kid. A car accident nearly a year ago had forced Will to take a long, hard look at his life—more importantly, at what he wanted to do with the rest of it. Cort was glad he'd decided to come back to the ranch. Although, looking at his brother now, he thought there was still a lot of that baseball player in Will's calculating expression. He figured there probably always would be.

The brothers were alike in a lot of ways, and different in others. They shared similar builds and hair color, and a mutual respect that had steadily grown over the past thirty years. Cort had been the first person to believe that his older brother would walk again. And when Will had decided to give up pro-ball once and for all, Cort had been the first to know.

Now, Will seemed to be trying to say something. Cort planned to listen. "How well do you think I know her?" he asked, keeping his voice low. "I slept with her, and she's going to have my child."

"But how well do you really know her?" Will asked. "More importantly, how well does she know you?"

A light seemed to come on over Cort's head. For the first time in days, he felt that old Sutherland grin replace his scowl. He didn't say anything for a long time, but his thoughts raced.

How well did Kimberly know him?

She'd been heaven in his arms that night in early February, but other than that, they'd hardly spoken. She'd come all the way to Nebraska to tell him she was carrying his child, and what had he done? Demanded that she marry him as if he were an arrogant jerk, that's what. No wonder she'd turned him down. After all, he hadn't exactly been his usual charming self.

"Will, you're a genius!" he declared, turning on his heel.

"Kimberly and Tommy are the geniuses," Will called to his back. "Hey, wait a minute. Aren't you going to tell me what you're going to do?"

Cort turned around. Swiping his hat off his head, he yelled, "Yee-ha! I'm not exactly sure about everything, but I have a few ideas, and I know exactly how I'm going to start."

"How's that?"

"Well, I'm just going to have to show Kimberly my better side."

Will assumed a stance similar to Cort's and slowly shook his head. "If she spent the night with you, she's already seen your better side."

Cort called his brother an irreverent name. Grinning crookedly, he said, "I'm talking about my other better side. Wish me luck."

"Good luck."

"Something tells me that, with Kimberly Wilson, I'm going to need it."

He turned around, quickly making his way toward his house at the end of the lane. Ideas filled his mind, plans taking shape with amazing speed. Yes, he probably *was* going to need a large dose of good luck where that blue-eyed genius was concerned.

But whether she knew it or not, so was she.

Chapter Three

"Cort!"

"Afternoon, Kimberly."

Kimberly opened the door cautiously, doing her best to shore her heart against Cort's lazy, masculine drawl. She didn't know what she was going to do about the sight of him standing there, his brown hat in one hand, a bouquet of daisies in the other.

Holding on to her composure, she said, "Will drove into North Platte about an hour ago. Krista's at work and Tommy's in school, so I'm the only one here."

"I know."

She felt her heart softening, her defenses beginning to subside. On some other level she'd known he probably wouldn't have bothered to shave for his brother, and Cort Sutherland didn't strike her as the type who bought spring flowers on a daily basis. But hearing him admit, in so many words, that he'd come to see *her* sent a warm glow through her.

He'd probably done a lot of thinking since she'd told him about the baby, but then, so had she. One of the downfalls of being in the genius category was that she could literally drive herself to distraction with the exorbitant detail with which she contemplated every possible problem, every possible angle, every possible course of action she might take. All her hours of thinking had led her to only one decision. No matter what happened, first and foremost, she was going to consider what was best for her baby.

Trying to keep her voice neutral, she asked, "What do you want, Cort?"

"I was hoping you'd take a walk with me."

"A walk?"

"You were right when you said I'd have a lot of questions once the shock wore off. Let's go for a walk. And talk."

Kimberly searched his expression and found more than she was looking for. There was an inherent determination in the set of his chin, and a hungry, almost lustful light in his eyes. Mixed with those, she saw a wistfulness she simply couldn't ignore. He *was* the father of her child, and he *did* deserve a few answers.

"A walk sounds nice. I'll just grab a jacket."

"Kimberly?"

She turned around again, and he slowly raised his right hand. "You can put these flowers in water if you'd like, or you can throw them away. Either way, I'll bring more for you tomorrow. Store-bought flowers are nice, but the prettiest flowers in the world are the ones that will be blooming right here come May. Of course, they won't be out for a week or two yet."

She hesitated, measuring him for a moment. As one second followed another, his expression changed in the subtlest of ways. Instinctively, she knew that his wide-eyed innocence was merely a smoke screen, and that he was still the same man who'd planted his feet on the ground last night and, in no uncertain terms, insisted that she marry him. But she still reacted to the eager affection coming from him.

After another moment of careful deliberation, she reached for the flowers. "I'll put these in water, Cort, but there's no need to bring more tomorrow. I'm not sure I'll be here then."

"Stay."

With a slight rising of her eyebrows, she said, "You know, for a question, that sounded suspiciously like a command."

"Please, Kim?"

Sunlight delineated his straight nose, the smooth, sure lines of his jaw and the shallow cleft in his chin. His features held a strong sensuality and so much pride it sent an ache to the area surrounding her heart. She turned away without answering, because she had no idea how to reply to the masculine entreaty in his voice. She didn't have enough experience dealing with men in general, let alone virile, roguish men like Cort Sutherland. What in the world was a woman supposed to do with a man like that?

She hurriedly placed the flowers in water and donned a lightweight navy jacket. By the time she joined him near the back door where he was waiting, she'd forced her nerves away.

"Now, about those questions you wanted to ask," she began, turning toward the barns.

Cort fell into step beside her, slowing his pace to match hers. She may have been staring straight ahead, but her no-nonsense attitude wasn't fooling him in the least. She didn't know what to make of his arrival this afternoon, or of his softly spoken plea. Not that he could blame her. Until a few minutes ago, he hadn't exactly been the epitome of politeness.

The questions Will had asked him this morning had hit home. Kimberly didn't know him, not really. They'd been great together in bed, but until yesterday, he'd known very little about her. He hadn't even known she loved coffee or chewed on her lower lip when she was nervous. He'd heard Krista mention her three older sisters a few times, but he couldn't recall anything specific. Kimberly probably knew even less about him. But all that was going to change. She was carrying his child, and he wanted her to know him in more than the biblical sense, although he had to admit, the thought of her lips on his stoked a gently growing fire all over again.

"So," he said, his voice deeper than it had been moments ago, "what do you think?"

Looking everywhere except at him, she said, "I think this entire area is lovely."

That wasn't what he meant, but he'd go along with her for now. Shrugging, he said, "I don't know if Krista told you or not, but the Sutherlands have only owned this portion of land for about a year. When my parents first started out thirty-odd years ago, they planned to make a living from cash cropping. After Will and I came along, they dreamed of passing the farm on to us. We knew early on that Will had his sights set on the major leagues, and although I liked farming, ranching was what I was itching to do. Luckily, we live on the edge of both worlds here in this part of Nebraska, and were able to combine the two. Dad claims the eastern five hundred acres of our land is the most fertile farmland between here and Lincoln. And the other fifteen hundred acres has some of the best prairie grass known to man or beast."

Kimberly hadn't intended to become so caught up in Cort's conversation, but she couldn't help it. His voice had taken on a new intensity that was impossible to ignore. Her instinctive response to him had always been powerful, but this was different, and even more invigorating.

They'd reached the corral where Socks, Tommy's new horse, was grazing on a tuft of grass growing on the outside of the fence. Resting her forearms on the top of the whitewashed gate nearby, she quietly said, "So your father expanded into ranching because you loved it?"

Cort made a sound that made both her and Socks glance up. "Oh, it wasn't quite that simple. You probably didn't know this, but we Sutherlands are a stubborn lot."

She rolled her eyes and shook her head at his wry expression, then waited for him to continue.

"I'm sure there were times when my parents had to bite their tongues to keep from telling Will and I how to live our lives. But they've both always understood about dreams. They encouraged Will and I to reach for our own stars. That process took Will to ball fields all over the country. Mine only took me to the other side of this section. If you'd like, I'd be happy to show you the entire operation. Of course, it's going to take some time to check out more than two thousand acres."

Kimberly felt his eyes on her, but didn't turn her head. This wasn't the first time he'd made a reference to her continued stay in Nebraska. His comments seemed innocent enough, but they still confused her. She'd decided to come to Nebraska because she'd needed to see Cort again, to see if what she felt for him was real. At the time, she hadn't thought beyond another meeting. Now she realized seeing him again and telling him about the baby had been but the tip of the iceberg. Seeing him again—more importantly, spending time with him—was opening her up to even more questions.

They moved on, strolling through the barn and on out the back door. After meandering along a narrow trail he called the lane, they stood at the edge of a field that would soon be cultivated and planted to corn. Pointing at a farmhouse a mile away, he said, "That's the house where Will and I grew up. And that," he said, turning in a complete circle, "is Sutherland land as far as the eye can see."

Kimberly couldn't imagine owning so much land. Nor could she imagine feeling as rooted to one place as Cort obviously did. She wondered what it would be like to belong to one corner of the world the way he did, as much a part of the land as the grass and fence posts themselves.

She was aware that Cort had gone down on his haunches next to her, but she couldn't take her eyes off the landscape directly in front of her. "Two thousand acres," she whispered, hearing the reverence in her own voice. "That's more than eighty-seven million square feet."

Cort glanced up, letting the soil he'd scooped into his hand sift through his fingers. Rising slowly, he clapped the dirt from his hands and asked, "Do you store that kind of information in your head?"

She glanced around sharply. Before his eyes, her face closed as if she'd let a secret that she'd been guarding slip.

"I just have a head for numbers, that's all. I think we should be getting back."

Once again, he fell into step beside her, but he wasn't ready to let the subject go. "How did you come up with that number?"

"Trust me, you don't really want to know."

"Yes I do."

"It's boring."

"Why don't you let me be the judge of that?"

She looked up at him as if searching his expression for the truth. He couldn't be sure if she found sincerity, or if she simply saw the stubborn streak he'd mentioned earlier, but after a time she started to speak.

"Well, you told me you own more than two thousand acres. I know there are a hundred and sixty square rods in one acre, which breaks down to four thousand eight hundred and forty square yards. I converted that number to square feet and multiplied by two thousand."

She made it sound like no big deal, but Cort happened to know better. Most people of average intelligence could have come up with that figure with the use of a calculator, a sheet of paper and a pencil. But Kimberly had figured it out in her head in an instant.

"If you ask me, that's pretty damned amazing."

"Like I said. I have a head for numbers. It's really nothing."

The tinge of pink on her cheeks reminded him of the way she'd looked that night more than two months ago when he'd first told her, his voice husky with desire, exactly what he wanted to do with her. His body tightened at the memory of how warm and languid and responsive she'd become in his arms, and of how quickly her throaty sighs had taken the place of her self-consciousness. He felt an almost overwhelming desire to banish her embarrassment all over again today.

"It looks as if we're back where we started."

The sound of her clipped voice drew him from his daydreams. He didn't know what there was about this woman that brought out his earthy instincts, but unless she could read his mind, she couldn't have known how profound her statement was. They *were* back at Will and Krista's where they'd started their walk, but that pulsing knot of longing he'd felt the first time he saw her was back, too.

Looking every place except at him, she said, "I'll keep you apprised of my decisions concerning the baby."

"Kimberly."

She glanced over her shoulder, one hand already on the doorknob. She made a sound that meant *what?* but it was obvious that she was anxious to get inside.

"I never got around to asking you those questions I mentioned earlier."

"What did you want to ask me, Cort?" she inquired, slowly turning around.

"I want you to stay."

"Why?"

"Because I want to get to know you better."

"You do?" she asked, her voice going all soft and shivery.

He nodded, not caring in the least that his hunger for her was written all over his face. "Will you stay?"

She tucked her lower lip between her teeth, then slowly whispered, "I'll think about it, Cort."

Her lips looked ever so pouty, her blue eyes wistful and dreamy. It sent the heat that was already thrumming through his bloodstream straight to the very center of him, blotting out every thought except one.

"Think about this, Kimberly."

He reached for her, loving the way the slender bones in her shoulders fit his hands. Strangely, he loved the inherent strength in the muscles beneath his fingers even more. Someday, he'd take the time to ask himself why, but right now he had more important things to do.

Drawing her closer, he lowered his face to hers, capturing her soft gasp in his own mouth. He'd only intended the kiss to last a moment, but it quickly spun out of control. Her lips parted beneath his, her breath mingling with his, her scent filling his nostrils, her touch filling him with greater need. This was the Kimberly he knew, amazingly gentle, yet urgent and responsive and so passionate she took his breath away.

Her jacket rasped beneath his hands as he molded her closer, her arms winding around his neck as if it was second nature. The movement brought her body in direct contact with his, her back arching, the kiss going on and on and on.

His lungs burned with the need for oxygen, and their mouths parted on a gasp for air. Breathing raggedly, he pressed his forehead to hers and finally said, "I'll be back later with those flowers."

His mouth curved into an unconscious smile. And then he turned on his heels and left, taking her gasp of surprise with him.

Kimberly lifted the gauzy white curtain aside, gazing into the backyard below where Tommy was frolicking with Blue, his big-footed black puppy. The boy was obviously trying to teach Blue some tricks, but the half-grown puppy seemed more intent upon nipping at Tommy's heels. Her nephew went down on his knees, then rolled onto his back in the grass, giggling for all he was worth at the wet kisses he received from Blue.

Still laughing, Tommy raised to his elbows and shook his head. A moment later, Kimberly understood why. Krista was walking toward him, a bright red jacket tucked in the crook of her arm. The second shake of the boy's head was firmer than the first. Undeterred, Krista held the jacket out in a manner that left little room for argument. Tommy donned the coat, but his expression let his mother know he was doing it for *her* benefit, not his own.

I wonder if my child will be anything like Tommy.

Kimberly let the curtain flutter back into place, feeling herself smile. Glancing away, she caught her reflection in the mirror across the room. Her shower-damp hair appeared a shade darker, the expression on her face as soft as her thoughts. Without realizing it, she'd placed one hand over her heart. The other was lovingly flattened against her abdomen.

The belt of her jade green robe was cinched tight around her waist. Turning this way and that, she searched for evidence that a baby was indeed growing inside her. Although her tummy might have been less flat than it was a month ago, the most visible sign of pregnancy was higher. She doubted she'd ever be large chested, but her breasts were fuller, more lush, and tender to the slightest touch.

I wonder if Cort will notice.

Biting her lip, she banished the thought and spread her fingers wide over her tummy, trying to imagine what it would be like to hold this baby in her arms. She still wasn't sure what she was going to do with the rest of her life, but she knew she was going to be the best mother she could possibly be. She'd already read several books on pregnancy and child care. Some people seemed to have premonitions regarding the gender of their children. Kimberly had absolutely no idea whether her baby was going to be a boy or a girl. She hoped it wasn't an indication that she was lacking maternal instincts in some elemental way. One thing she knew she wasn't lacking was love for this tiny child.

She didn't know where the love came from, but it was all-consuming and awe-inspiring. It was at once fierce and gentle, and different from anything she'd ever felt before.

Tucking her lower lip between her teeth, she tried to imagine what the baby would look like. Would this little being be blond and fair like her? Or would the child have dark hair and bronze skin like Cort? If she raised her child far away from here, would any similarities in appearance to Cort haunt her as long as she lived?

She turned away from the mirror, forcing herself not to think about being haunted by memories. Think about something else, she told herself.

Think about this, Kimberly.

The words Cort had whispered moments before he'd kissed her rippled through her mind the way an echo rolled through a deep canyon. She'd told him she'd think about staying in Nebraska. *And then he kissed me senseless.*

Her hands flew to her face, her fingers covering her lips. It had been hours since it had happened, but she was still reeling from that kiss.

"Kimberly," Krista called from the bottom of the stairway. "Cort's here."

Coming out of her stupor, she called, "Thanks, Krista. Tell him I'll be right down."

Like a woman on a mission, she strode to the closet and took out a pair of fawn brown slacks and matching lightweight sweater. Donning the clothes with deft movements, her thoughts cleared. Nearly two and a half months ago she'd made a vow to take charge of her own life. Lately, she hadn't been keeping it very well. That was about to change.

She added a delicate gold chain and matching earrings, brushed her hair, which was almost dry now, then surveyed her face. Unfortunately, she hadn't been blessed with dark eyebrows and lashes like Krista's. Her pale cheeks and eyelashes made her look vulnerable. Since this was no time to appear weak in any way, she reached for her mascara and blush.

Cort had asked her a very important question today. He'd asked her to stay. The mere thought made her giddy, because it was what she truly wanted to do. But this wasn't a decision she could make lightly. She'd never been a person who flew by the seat of her pants, and this was hardly the time to start. She had another life to consider now, and some incredibly important decisions to make regarding her child's welfare.

She remembered how Cort had reacted when she'd first told him about the baby. He'd insisted that she marry him, saying he wanted the baby to have two parents. Deep inside, that's what she wanted, too. But she wanted more than a shotgun wedding or a marriage of convenience. She wanted Cort to love her. She didn't see how there was any chance of that happening if she went back to Boston. Maybe, just maybe, the two of them could build a lasting relationship. If she stayed.

Or maybe he'll break my heart.

The thought came, unbidden, but crystal clear. Taking a deep breath for courage, she glanced in the mirror, surveying her reflection from head to toe. Satisfied that she'd done everything in her power to fortify her appearance and her resolve, she held her head high and headed for the stairs.

"I just came from Dad's place."

Keeping one eye trained on the stairway, Cort said, "Don't tell me. He happened to mention the word *drought*, right?"

"Every other word," Will said from his position on the floor where he was pretending to arm wrestle with Tommy, who had just come in from outside. "Evidently, the *Farmer's Almanac* is predicting a drier than normal season. Dad says there's no sense planting until it rains."

Cort cast his brother a sardonic look. Joe Sutherland had started talking about a drought in March. It was true that there had been a surprisingly low amount of snow over the winter, and although they'd had a few April showers, this neck of Nebraska was definitely low on its annual water fall. Cort didn't believe there was cause for concern. Yet.

"Might as well just save ourselves a lot of trouble and throw in the towel," Will said, shaking his head.

"And let nature and the bank fight over what's left of our land," the brothers said in unison, mimicking their father.

"You two be nice," Krista said over the top of the magazine she was reading.

"We're always nice," Will answered with a wink.

Cort couldn't help noticing the warm expression that passed between Will and Krista, and suddenly felt in the way. He settled himself more comfortably against the doorframe, wondering what was taking Kimberly so long. He imagined her standing in front of the closet in one of the many spare bedrooms in this big old house, thoughtfully choosing an outfit. He'd watched her dress in the wee hours of that morning all those weeks ago, and could easily picture her the same way right now. Only today her smooth pale skin wouldn't be red in places where his whisker stubble had chafed.

He cleared his throat, trying to remember what he and Will had been talking about. Oh, yeah. Their father.

They'd both grown accustomed to Joe Sutherland's constant worrying. It came with the territory. If nature didn't taunt them with droughts, it threatened them with floods or bottomed-out beef prices.

Tommy slammed Will's arm to the table and noisily declared himself the winner. Laughing, the little boy said, "No matter what the elements throw our way, we'll plant our crops and herd our cattle, right, Daddy?"

"Come hell or high..." Cort turned his head, his voice trailing off in mid-sentence.

Kimberly was standing on the bottom step, looking directly at him. She hadn't made a sound, yet he'd somehow known she was there. Was it his imagination, or was there something different about her tonight? Her hair was long and loose, her clothing trendy and expensive. Nothing unusual about that. But there *was* something different about her. He just couldn't quite put his finger on what had changed.

"Hello, Cort."

It was the first time she'd spoken to him since he'd kissed her this afternoon. He wanted to kiss her all over again.

"Why does Uncle Cort look so funny?"

Cort heard Tommy's question, and although it reminded him that Will and Krista and Tommy were still in the room, he paid them little attention. Ambling closer, he said, "Evenin', Kimberly. These are for you."

"Cort, flowers aren't necessary."

"There's one thing you should know about me. I'm a man of my word."

Either the wind had picked up and was howling through the eaves, or else Tommy, Will and Krista all let their breath out in little gusts. Ignoring them, he asked, "What do you say we go someplace a little more private?"

"Were you thinking of taking another walk?"

"Or we could go for a ride. I could show you a few of the local attractions. There's the Scouts Rest Ranch where Buffalo Bill lived near North Platte. Or we could drive on down to Gotherburg and see an authentic Pony Express Station."

"Maybe another time."

He watched her closely, wondering if she was aware of what she'd just implied. "Does this mean you've decided to stay?"

"I want to talk to you about that."

Suddenly, he understood what was different about Kim tonight. She wasn't blushing, and she wasn't stammering. She looked as if she knew her own mind, and knew exactly what she wanted. Was it his imagination, or did the light in her eyes mean she wanted *him?*

With anticipation slowing his thoughts, he said, "I'd be happy to show you those attractions another time. And I think it would be best if we discussed this in private."

She wet her lips in a way that made his heart pound and slowly stepped around him. He thought he saw her wink at Krista, and he was sure his sister-in-law answered with a sly grin.

So, he thought to himself, the sisters had been talking about him. Another time he might not have appreciated that, but after the way Kimberly had kissed him this afternoon, she could talk about him to her heart's content.

She glanced over her shoulder when she reached the doorway and quickly surveyed the room. "Are you coming, Cort?"

Without waiting for his reply, she opened the door and stepped through.

"You'd better do what she says, Uncle Cort, if you know what's good for you."

Cort glanced at Will and Krista, and then at Tommy. Feeling his adrenaline kick in and that old Sutherland grin slide into place, he winked at his one and only nephew and said, "Thanks, partner. I think I'll do just that."

Kimberly heard the door close and knew without turning around that Cort had followed her outside. It was cooler now that the sun had gone down, but it wasn't the night air that made goose bumps dance up and down her spine. Nerves were responsible for that. Nerves, and Cort Sutherland.

Gravel ground beneath his boots, each crunch measuring his long-legged stride. Feeling the need to move, she set off in the same direction they'd taken that afternoon, willing her mind to clear. She was proud of the way she'd handled herself inside, but before she lost her nerve, she knew she couldn't wait too long to ask him a few questions.

"Nice night," he said, walking beside her.

"Beautiful." She supposed it was true, but with so much on her mind, she wouldn't have cared if it had been threatening to snow.

"Now that you have me to yourself, what are you going to do with me?"

She glanced up at him sharply, then shook her head at his cocky half smile. *"Pu-lease."*

"Why don't we go for that drive I mentioned?"

They'd reached his brown Ford, but rather than move to get in, she turned and faced him. "If I asked you a question, would you promise to be completely honest with me?"

Drawing a step closer, he dipped his head as if to see her better in the gathering darkness. "This sounds serious,

Kimberly, but maybe I can save you a little trouble. If you're worried about some other woman, don't be. I'm not seeing anyone else right now. I haven't in a long time."

His declaration wrapped around her like strong arms and a warm smile. She would have liked to ask him if the women around here were blind, but knew this wasn't the time or the place. Storing the question for another day, she said, "That's nice, Cort, but that isn't what I was going to ask. What I wanted to know is this. What, exactly, are your intentions?"

"My intentions?" he asked, taking another step closer. As if someone slowly turned a knob, his eyelashes dropped lower, and so did his voice. Reaching for her, he whispered, "I'd rather show you."

She took one step back and another to the side, effectively sidestepping his advance. "Cort, you aren't making this easy for me."

"Honey, I'm trying to make it as easy as possible."

She felt herself softening, her resolve turning to liquid. Giving herself a mental shake, she said, "Once again, we're not talking about the same thing."

"Do you really want to know my intentions?" he asked, moving ever closer. "They're simple. I intend to convince you to marry me."

Her lips parted slightly, her eyes opening wide. "But you don't even know me."

"You wanted the truth. There it is. I could have lied, but it's not my style. I suppose I could have waited to tell you, but I'd rather get started convincing you."

The sun was gone, and the stars had yet to shine. But Cort didn't seem to need any other source of light. His eyes were filled with his own special glimmer, his hands resting comfortably on his hips. His shoulders were broad but relaxed, his stance wide legged and so loose jointed that he could have stepped from the pages of an old western novel.

She wondered where he could have gotten so much calm self-assurance when she'd gone nearly thirty-one years with almost none. Reminding herself of her vow, she held on to every ounce of determination she possessed and quietly said, "You sound awfully sure of yourself."

"What can I say? I'm a Sutherland, and we Sutherlands are good at what we do."

"Are all Sutherlands braggers, too?"

He shrugged, but he didn't grin as she'd expected. Instead, he looked directly into her eyes and said, "It ain't braggin' if you can really do it."

Her heart beat heavy in her chest. This time, when he reached for her hand, she didn't move. She couldn't.

Smoothing a work-roughened thumb across her palm, he leaned closer and asked, "Are you sure you wouldn't like to go for a drive with me, Kim? Maybe to my place?"

Thanking whatever deity that was responsible for allowing her some semblance of rationality and self-preservation, she shook her head and took a backward step. "I think it might be best to save that until tomorrow."

He stared into her eyes for a long time. Just when she was sure he wasn't going to say anything ever again, he said, "All right, Kimberly. I'll wait if I have to. But I will convince you to marry me."

She didn't answer. And when he began to lower his mouth to hers, she didn't move.

Her heart pounded an erratic rhythm, her breathing all but ceasing as she waited for his kiss. His lips touched hers, but softer, gentler, than ever before. Instead of the passion of his last kiss, this was but a whisper against her lips, a soft, tender brush of his mouth against hers. A promise of what was to come.

Beginning tomorrow.

Chapter Four

Kimberly pulled into Cort's driveway and came to a stop near the house. A painted metal chair sat at a cockeyed angle on the porch, but nothing else was amiss. There was no movement inside, and the doors were all closed tight.

She stepped from the car and looked around, trying to decide what to do. It didn't look as if Cort was home, not that she was surprised. After all, it was ten o'clock in the morning, and he wasn't expecting her until five.

She'd been in Nebraska a week, and ever since she'd told Cort that she'd stay awhile, he'd been on his best behavior. She could see that spring was an extremely busy time on the ranch, yet he'd taken hours away from his chores to spend time with her. He'd wooed her and courted her, holding doors, and holding her gaze.

True to his word, he'd taken her to see some of the sights in and around North Platte. She'd truly enjoyed the time she spent with Cort, not to mention the excursions they'd taken. Until these past few days, she hadn't thought of Nebraska as a western state. But after driving over the very land that thousands of covered wagons had followed on their journey westward to places as far away as Oregon and Washington, she understood why Cort referred to Nebraska as the land where the west began.

Glancing around, she took in the old white house and its crooked porch. She'd been here before, twice, but each time had been at night. And each time she'd had things other than her surroundings on her mind.

She and Cort had plans to go out to dinner tonight, but that was still hours and hours away. Never one to be able to sit idle for long, she'd tried to help Krista with housework this morning, and ended up getting in the way. When Krista happened to mention that she needed a few things in North Platte, Kimberly had jumped at the chance to help out. According to the map, North Platte was only thirty miles away. While she was there, she planned to run a few errands of her own.

She wasn't sure why she'd driven to Cort's place first, but now that she was here, her natural curiosity was taking over. Surely, there wouldn't be any harm in taking a little stroll.

Following the gravel driveway around the side of the house, she saw several low outbuildings and a big weathered barn. She poked her head inside a couple of the buildings. Finding hay in one and some sort of machinery in the other, she continued on toward the fence surrounding the barn. Two horses glanced up as she approached, but it was a soft "Maaa" that drew her around to the back of the barn.

A small brown calf instantly limped over to the gate, lowing forlornly. Kimberly glanced around for its mother, but no other cows were in sight.

"Aren't you the sweetest thing?"

The calf looked at her cross-eyed, then shyly lowered her long, curly lashes. Kimberly was lost. She'd never been around farm animals, but she reached her hand tentatively over the gate and stroked that little head, surprised at how knotty it felt underneath the brown fuzzy covering of hair.

The calf ate up the attention, turning her head this way and that. Chuckling, Kimberly said, "That's the last time I'm going to believe everything I read. I thought cattle were supposed to be a little on the, well, on the dull-minded side. Why, you're as bright as they come, aren't you? Now what are you doing here all by yourself?"

"She got trampled a couple of days ago."

Kimberly jerked around, her hand flying to her throat, her sudden movement startling another "Maaa" out of the little calf. "Oh, Mr. Sutherland. I didn't know you were there."

"You seemed to be pretty engrossed in that little gal."

She wanted to search the older Sutherland's face for hidden meaning, but her eyes wouldn't seem to cooperate. Wishing she could banish her shyness once and for all, she forced her gaze back to his and said, "I hope you don't mind my snooping around."

Joe Sutherland looked at her long and hard for a moment, then slowly removed his hat. "Course I don't mind. It's only natural that you'd be curious about this place. After all, it is where the man who asked you to marry him lives. So tell me, young lady. What do you think of the old place so far?"

In Boston, thirty-year-old women tended to get testy when a man of any age called them "young lady." Today, Kimberly felt strangely touched.

"I think it's very interesting," she answered honestly.

He slapped the dust from his cowboy hat the way she'd seen Cort do, then casually toyed with the rim. Joe Sutherland's hair was thinning on top, but his face was shaped by strong lines and masculine hollows just like Cort's. There was a shallow cleft in his chin that was a dead ringer for his son's, but the look in his eyes could have only come from living.

"Cort tells me you're from Boston. I was there a couple of years ago to watch Will play ball. Won that game, too. Eight to zip."

Kimberly nodded and smiled.

"Nice town, if you like big cities. Do you?" he asked. "Like big cities, I mean."

She'd been spending a great deal of time with Cort these past few days, but she'd seen next to nothing of his parents. Consequently, she wasn't sure how they felt about her intrusion into their son's life. She needn't have worried. Joe Sutherland appeared to have a great deal of inborn class and social grace. She could hardly blame him for the fact that he was curious about her.

She continued to pet the calf behind her back, smiling to herself when the little dickens butted her hand. "Big cities, small towns, the country. I suppose they all have their good qualities. But it's the people we surround ourselves with that really matter. Don't you agree?"

He narrowed his eyes, then placed his hat back on his head. "I couldn't have said it better myself. I hope you don't mind, but there's something else I've been wantin' to say, too. Cort's a good man, Kimberly. He's as steadfast as they come. Both my boys are driven. I'm convinced it's what made Will get up out of that wheelchair last year. And it's what's made this ranch a successful operation, too."

They both turned their heads at the sound of a horse approaching. With his eyes trained on the rider, Joe continued. "Now, I admit they're both a little stubborn, but I wouldn't change them, that's for sure. And I can't see how any woman could do much better than either of my boys."

Cort swung down off his horse, his arrival saving her from having to answer. Looping the reins loosely in one hand, he looked at his father and slowly said, "Are you flirting with my date, Dad?"

"No crime against talking, son. But don't tell your mother, just the same."

He winked at Kimberly. "Think about what I said, young lady."

"I will, Mr. Sutherland. I promise."

He started to walk away, then stopped. "Oh, and one more thing. My friends call me Joe. Since you're going to be my daughter-in-law, it seems only fitting that you do, too."

He grinned at her as if he knew full well that he'd successfully disarmed her with his last statement, then slowly sauntered away. Kimberly suddenly understood several things about the Sutherland men, one in particular. The fact that Cort was arrogant at times and had a tendency to brag was no fluke. He'd come by those things from a very direct route. Straight from his father. He'd obviously come by his sexy swagger and inborn charm the same way.

"And here I thought I'd be the first to know."

She glanced at Cort in confusion. One look at the cocky angle of his chin and understanding dawned. Letting out a little huff of air, she said, "And here *I* thought *I'd* be the first to know."

Cort ambled closer. Tipping his hat up slightly, he said, "Well, it looks like you've won another Sutherland over."

"You think so?"

"I know so. But tell me something, Kimberly. Aren't you a little early for dinner?"

If she would have been anyone else, she might have cuffed him in the arm. Torn by conflicting wishes—one that she could be more playful and fun, and the other that Cort could love her exactly the way she was—she shrugged, then slid her hands into the deep pockets of her burgundy silk jacket.

"I have to run a few errands for Krista. But I was hoping you'd show me around the ranch first."

"Couldn't stay away, huh?"

Shrugging and shaking her head in a gesture of innocence, she said, "You already have the self-confidence of ten men, so don't expect me to add to the swelling of your head. But I do hope you don't mind the interruption."

"Do I look crazy, Kim?"

Man, he could turn her inside out with just a look, but when he called her *Kim,* his voice all deep and dewy, her knees went weak and her mind turned to mush. No, he didn't look crazy. He looked rugged, and virile, and sure of himself. And of her. Therein lay the problem. She didn't want him to be sure of her. She wanted him to be in love with her.

The calf nudged her hand again, wanting attention. "Feisty little thing."

"I beg your pardon?" he asked.

It felt good to be the one grinning knowingly for a change. Gesturing toward the gate at her back, she said, "I was referring to the calf. Your father said she'd been trampled."

She turned around, and Cort walked up to the gate. Resting one forearm on the top board, he stroked the calf's nose with two long, blunt-tipped fingers. "Found her a few days ago bawling all by her lonesome out in the middle of the sand hills."

"What happened to her mother?"

"She didn't make it."

Kimberly bit her lip. "Aw. The poor baby. What's her name?"

"Her name?"

"Yes. You know. What do you call her?"

"I call her a six-week-old Brangus calf."

"You mean she doesn't *have* a name? Why, that's horrible."

"She's not a pet, Kimberly. We herd hundreds of cattle each year. It's how I make my living. We raise them, feed them and then we sell them. Some of the best steaks in the country get their start right here on the Sutherland ranch."

Kimberly's stomach had been feeling churlish all morning, but what she was experiencing right now was worse than morning sickness. Cort planned to sell this precious baby for... for... for slabs of meat? Her insides roiled like a turbulent sea. Placing one hand over her mouth, she glanced down at the calf and took a backward step.

Cort caught a movement out of the corner of his eye and turned around to look at Kimberly. Every last speck of color had drained from her face, and she looked on the verge of being sick. Thinking fast, he placed himself between her and the calf and gently nudged her in another direction.

"Whoa," he said, close to her ear. "I think it might be a good idea to begin the tour of the ranch someplace else, don't you?"

She nodded, her hand falling away from her lips.

Reaching for his horse's reins, he said, "Come on, Rambler. Let's show Kimberly where you live."

He caught her brief glance at his palomino, and her subsequent critical squint. "Horses have names. Cattle don't. Sounds fair. If you're a horse."

Cort opened his eyes wide, then narrowed them. Within seconds, a smile found its way to his lips. A curious swooping pulled at his insides. If he wasn't mistaken, he'd just been duly chastised. It had been done so subtly he would have missed it if he hadn't been paying close attention. Few women could have pulled it off with so much dignity, but then, few women would have tried.

He knew his way around the ranch without looking, which was a good thing because he couldn't take his eyes off Kimberly. Her hands were stuffed in the pockets of the softest-looking jacket he'd ever laid eyes on, her long legs ensconced in elegant-looking trousers. It was hardly the kind of outfit a person wore on a ranch, but she didn't seem to care. She was staring straight ahead, so all he could see was her profile, but it was enough. Her skin had a little color again, her pert nose and proud chin raised at a haughty angle. God, he loved it when she went all saucy and insolent on him. It sent something intense flaring through him. When it stopped just below his belt, his thoughts started down a different path entirely.

He'd always believed he'd find a good woman and settle down like his parents had, and like Will had a few months ago. But in his imagination, the woman he ended up with would be from Nebraska. She'd know you couldn't name your next meal, and she'd understand how the weather affected a rancher's mood. She sure as hell wouldn't wear silk for a tour of the barns and machinery. He'd dated several women from the area, women who were bright, women who'd worn blue jeans and dabbed perfume underneath the collars of their cotton shirts. But not one of them could make him smile in the middle of the morning the way Kimberly did. Not one of them could ignite his desire so quickly and so thoroughly, either.

And not one of them was carrying his child.

"Do you call this the paddock?"

Her question brought him, at least partially, to his senses. This was the middle of the day, and they were in the middle of an area that could be seen from just about any building within a hundred yards. As if to prove his point, raised voices came from the other side of the bunkhouse. A door slammed, and three of his best cowhands squinted as they stepped into the bright April sun.

Slipping a hand around Kimberly's waist, he veered to the right and said, "Some people call it a paddock. But around here, we call it the corral. Now, how would you like to meet a few of the men?"

Kimberly glanced up at Cort in surprise. His voice was always filled with intensity when he talked about his ranch, but it had a way of dipping even lower when he was thinking about kissing her. It had been that low a moment ago, so low that she'd been anticipating being drawn into his arms and thoroughly kissed.

"Hey, fellas," Cort called. "Wait up. There's someone here I'd like you to meet."

Three heads turned sharply, followed by three rangy pairs of shoulders. Two of the men spat, and the third one, the youngest, nudged them both.

As the men ambled closer on legs bowed in varying degrees, Cort said, "Mo, Frank, Pokey, I'd like you to meet Kimberly Wilson. Kimberly, my three best cowhands."

"Hello," Kimberly said. "It's nice to meet you."

"Aw, shucks. Um, hello, ma'am."

"Er, it's nice to meetchoo, too, miss."

"That's right. Real nice."

Kimberly managed to keep a serene smile on her face, but just barely. The last man who'd spoken—Cort had called him Frank—didn't look a day over seventeen. Mo was probably close to her age, but the man named Pokey was a different story. His whiskers were gray, his face deeply lined, the knuckles of his hands gnarled and covered with skin that looked as tough as leather.

She smiled at each of them in turn and said, "Cort tells me you three are his best cowhands."

Three pairs of eyes darted to hers, then slipped away again.

"Er, guess we'd better see to those fences," Mo stammered.

"You're right. You're absolutely right," Pokey said, his voice as gravelly as any she'd ever heard.

"Well, time's a wastin'," Frank added.

"Yep. Gotta go."

Just like that, all three men turned on the heels of their worn cowboy boots and hurried away as fast as their legs would take them.

"I don't get it." Cort was staring straight ahead, watching them go.

"What do you mean?" she asked.

"Those men are usually as happy as cattle in corn at the mere sight of a pretty woman."

For the life of her, Kimberly didn't know why she suddenly felt shy. Still, Cort's compliment worked over her in waves. He thought she was pretty. Not attractive. Not nice looking. Pretty.

Suddenly, she became aware of the fresh breeze fluttering through her hair. The air smelled faintly of sunshine, of wide open spaces and of spring. It seemed fitting somehow that she felt like a flower opening its petals for the first time.

"They know about the baby, don't they?" she asked quietly.

"What do you mean?"

"I don't know how to say this properly. I just thought there was probably a reason why they all looked as if they'd just found themselves at their own funerals."

He stiffened, staring straight ahead. "I'll talk to them. I won't have them making you feel ill at ease. If they can't handle it, I'll fire them."

"Cort, I'm sure that won't be necessary."

"I'll be the judge of that!"

"No, really. Don't fire them on my account. I mean, they seemed nice enough. And you're the one who said they're your best cowhands. I'll bet they've walked the extra mile for you more than once. They're just surprised, that's all. They're probably used to living by the code of the west and all that."

"Yeah," he said reluctantly. "You're probably right." After a long silence, he added, "Are you sure you're all right?"

She grinned at him then. She couldn't help it. He'd looked as if he'd gladly beat up anyone who looked askance at her or her condition. He wanted to protect her, and he thought she was pretty. Sometimes, she thought it was possible that he might even come to love her.

Raising her face to the sky, she closed her eyes and smiled into the breeze. "Of course I'm all right. In fact, I don't think I've ever been better. Now, how about the rest of that tour you promised me?"

His eyes homed in on her mouth, and his expression darkened. Again, she thought he might kiss her. Instead, he slapped his hands to his hips and tipped his chin at a lofty angle. "One personalized tour coming right up, ma'am. If you'll just walk this way."

Assuming the stance she'd used a million times in the business world, one hand tucked around her waist, the other cupping her chin, she observed his loose-jointed swagger. Since she was pretty sure she couldn't walk that way without hurting herself, she shook her head and followed.

"Thanks for the guided tour, Cort."

"My pleasure."

They were standing next to the car, her on one side of the open door, him on the other. His eyes had taken on that sleepy glint that didn't necessarily mean he was sleepy. Letting her gaze drop to his mouth, then slowly climb back to his eyes, she said, "No, I mean it. I can't believe how much a person has to know in order to run a successful ranching operation. There are things you told me today I could never learn from a textbook, although I think I might hunt up a library in North Platte and check out a few books just for fun."

"Can I make a suggestion?"

The fact that he'd *asked* gave her pause. Trying to shrug in an offhand manner, she said, "Of course."

"As soft and elegant as you look in that outfit, maybe you could buy a pair of jeans and a cotton shirt for your next guided tour."

Kimberly had never owned a plain old pair of jeans in her life. Her casual clothes consisted of wool trousers, designer jeans, knit leggings and softly colored tunics, jackets and sweaters. She glanced down at her outfit, wondering how it looked to Cort. There hadn't been a hint of disapproval in his voice a moment ago. In fact, *soft* and *elegant* were words that suggested male appreciation, and sent that warm, feather-down softness to her knees.

An engine started up in one of the outbuildings. Seconds later, Pokey and Frank emerged in a muddy Jeep, bumping over potholes on their way down the lane. Watching their progress, she said, "Jeans, hmm? I might just do that in North Platte today. And while I'm there, I'm going to look for a place of my own."

"Now why would you want to go and do that?"

The sudden change in Cort's tone of voice drew her attention back to him. Eyeing him cautiously, she said, "Krista and Will have been wonderful, but they're newlyweds. I walked in on an extremely passionate kiss this morning, and it wasn't the first time. I can't stay with them indefinitely, Cort, no matter how welcome they've made me feel."

"North Platte is thirty miles away."

"I've commuted farther than that in Boston."

"You're not in Boston. You're here."

Why did he sound so angry? "There aren't exactly a lot of apartments or condos out here," she said softly.

"I know of a place you could stay, free of charge, for the rest of your life."

She stared into his eyes. Waiting. Wishing. Hoping.

Say you love me, she whispered inside her head. *And I'll marry you in an instant, Cort.*

He didn't say anything, just stood there glaring at her through narrowed eyes.

When Kimberly couldn't stand the silence another second, she said, "We've been over this before, several times. We still don't know each other nearly well enough to think about marriage in a serious manner."

He leaned closer and quietly said, "I will convince you to marry me, Kimberly. You wait and see."

She raised her eyebrows, then lowered them. With a slight shake of her head, she said, "I know, I know. It isn't bragging if you can really do it."

"See that?" he asked. "You know me better than you think already."

All she could do was shake her head at his wry expression.

"Oh," he said, "there's one more thing."

His hand shot out and his mouth lowered to hers. It happened fast, but she still should have seen it coming.

His lips moved coaxingly over hers, sending her heart into a tailspin straight to her stomach. She could have backed away. He wasn't holding her, except where their fingers were entwined and where his mouth touched hers. But she didn't want to back away. She closed her eyes dreamily, telling herself she'd be on the lookout for similar tactics at a later date. Right now, she might as well enjoy the surprise.

"Aunt Kimberly?"

Kimberly stopped at the end of the hall and backtracked, coming to a stop in the doorway of a room decorated with cowboys and baseball players. "Whatcha need, Tommy?"

"I'm having a hard time finding the trajectory angle and the time and place of the next window so I can bring my spaceship back to Earth."

She walked into the room and leaned down, peering over the top of her nephew's head. Scanning the digits and figures in the corner of the computer screen, she said, "Type in your outer quadrants. Now push your control key. There, see the data on the screen? Use those numbers to figure the trajectory angle."

She waited until the boy had pressed the proper keys. "Push the control key again. See? The computer's calculating for you. Now, type in the date and time."

Tommy did as she instructed. The computer hummed for several seconds, then bleeped three times. The screen turned black, then bright yellow. Tommy grinned, and Kimberly said, "Voilà! You just found your window and are about to reenter the Earth's atmosphere."

"Cool."

She peered around so that she could look at Tommy's face. She could see the reflection of the computer's screen in his round brown eyes. He was such a genius. His expression remained intent, his fingers punching numbers on the keyboard in front of him.

"Mmm. You smell good."

She felt her eyes widen, but his remained on the screen. He may have been a genius, but he was also well on his way to being a *man*.

"Why, thank you," she said, unable to resist the opportunity to ruffle his dark hair.

"Why do girls wear perfume?"

Although he still wasn't looking at her, she was no longer fooled into believing he wasn't aware of her every move. "Well," she answered, "I suppose we wear perfume because we want to smell nice."

"Do you want to smell nice because you're going out to dinner with Uncle Cort?"

"I suppose."

"Why?"

Now what was she supposed to say?

"Mom told me you're going to have a baby."

His gaze was now fixed on her. She wet her lips, then softened them with a smile and said, "That's right, Tommy. I am."

"And Uncle Cort is the daddy."

Alarms began to sound on the computer. Tommy's spaceship was about to blow up during reentry. Similar alarms were going off inside Kimberly's head.

Tommy let his eyes trail off to the havoc taking place on the computer screen, but he made no move to punch any buttons. "I heard Pokey and Mo talking earlier today. They didn't know I was listening, but they said that Uncle Cort wants you to marry him, but you haven't decided what you're going to do."

"That's right."

"Why? You like Uncle Cort, don'tcha? I mean, you must like him if you made a baby with him."

She'd gotten into *why* trouble with Tommy before, but never as deeply and thoroughly as she was right now. While she struggled with the question, he asked another.

"Why don't you just marry him?"

Just how could she explain the situation to this child who was older than his actual years in some respects, but still a little boy in others? For the life of her, she didn't know how to reply.

They both looked at the screen where the spaceship was now engulfed in flames. Keeping her voice quiet, she said, "It's not that simple, Tommy. I wish it was, but it isn't. It's a little bit like flying that spaceship. There's a lot to think about."

Letting her gaze trail over the fancy computer system, she said, "That's a neat computer game. Did your mother buy it for you?"

"Nope. My dad did. I know he isn't really my dad. I mean, he isn't my biological father, but I love him a lot. He loves me, too, so much that he's adopting me. I just think you should marry Uncle Cort so your baby won't have to wait until he's seven years old to have a dad."

Tears stung Kimberly's eyes. It might have been the result of hormones, or it might have been the fact that this beautiful child loved her enough to offer his advice. Pressing a kiss to his smooth cheek, she smiled through the haze of tears and said, "You're pretty terrific, do you know that? And just between you and me, I'll take your suggestion under advisement."

"Cool. Now, I'd better get back to my game. NASA's not going to be very happy, because I'm going to need another spaceship. Oh, and Aunt Kimberly?"

She turned at the door. "Hmm?"

"You really do smell good. I'm sure Uncle Cort will notice."

Her hands fell to her sides. She stared at the back of Tommy's head for a few seconds, thinking that it was amazing. The child had only been a Sutherland for a few months, but his cocky self-confidence was already a carbon copy of his Uncle Cort's.

"Mmm. You even smell beautiful."

Kimberly looked at Cort, his eyes darkening to the color of the sky just before rain.

"You're the second male to tell me that today."

He was standing in his driveway, one hand on the door handle of his truck, the other extended to help her to the ground. "Should I be jealous?"

"That's entirely up to you. The first one was seven years old."

"Ah. Tommy's a smart kid."

She placed her fingers on his palm and slid to her feet. Rather than stepping back to allow her more room, he stayed where he was, so that they ended up face-to-face, thigh-to-thigh.

"The moon's full tonight," he said, his voice going all deep and husky. "What do you say we take a little stroll, and you can tell me what else you did in North Platte today."

The dome light cast shadows across his features, but it couldn't hide the sensuous glimmer in his eyes. He'd been this way all evening, roguish one second, coaxing the next. The man was wreaking havoc with her senses, just as he'd undoubtedly intended. Not that she was making it entirely easy for him in return.

"In North Platte?" she asked, feigning innocence so poorly she almost smiled.

"Yes," he countered. "In North Platte. You did say you were going there today."

Kimberly closed the lapels of her soft jacket with her free hand, then slipped her fingers into her pocket. This wasn't the first time he'd mentioned her excursion into North Platte today, nor was it the first time she'd failed to give him the answer he was waiting for. He wanted to know if she'd found a place to stay. Sometime before the evening was over, she'd have to tell him.

Gently pulling her hand from his, she stepped around him and tipped her face toward the sky. "As I mentioned earlier, there really isn't that much to tell. I picked up a few groceries for Krista, and a new computer game for Tommy. I went to the post office for stamps, and searched for something or other Will needed from the hardware store. Oh, I guess I did do something else."

"What's that?"

"I bought this pair of blue jeans. I found them in the neatest little shop downtown."

"Did you see any other interesting sights? Any buildings that caught your eye?"

"A few."

Cort's groan momentarily drowned out the sound of his rapidly beating heart. One glance at the coy little smile on Kimberly's lips told him she knew exactly what she was doing. Not only that, she was enjoying herself immensely. Interestingly enough, so was he.

Although he hadn't been able to coax her into coming clean about her search for an apartment, he couldn't deny his growing attraction to this woman. She'd fastened her hair on top of her head, but it seemed that those blond tendrils were about as cooperative as she was. Golden pins held some of the hair into place, but the rest tumbled loose around her ears, forehead and neck, looking pleasantly mussed, and sexy as hell.

They'd just come from the Stapleton Steak House. Sitting in the dimly lit booth, she'd studied the menu for an inordinate amount of time. After muttering something about sloe-eyed babies, she'd calmly yet firmly ordered a turkey sandwich on whole-wheat bread.

Cort had hid his own smile behind his menu at the discomfited expression on the young waitress's face. Not that he could blame the poor girl. Kimberly Wilson was probably the only person who'd ever ordered a turkey sandwich at the best steak house in the county. She got her sandwich, but judging from the amount of time it took to arrive, he'd bet his best horse that someone had made a quick run to the grocery store for the turkey cold cuts. He wondered if Kimberly had always avoided red meat, or if her aversion to beef was a result of her fascination with the little Brangus calf she'd befriended this morning.

The moon had just begun to glow when they'd pulled out of the parking lot in Stapleton. Now it was full and so bright it threw shadows behind them. She stopped walking when she reached the old shed, and sank onto a weathered bench attached to one end. Looking up at the sky, she said, "Not a cloud in sight."

Cort settled his body next to hers, feeling the coolness of the wood seep through his thin jacket. "Will and I always said spring was our favorite time of the year. There's just something about the sky and the air and the grass right now. Most kids want to camp out in the summertime. Will and I always begged to do it in the spring. I remember the first time we talked Mom and Dad into letting us stay outside all night. We were probably eight and nine years old. We spent all evening long hauling our gear from the house. We pitched a tent, rolled out sleeping bags, searched underneath our beds for batteries for our flashlights, filled a thermos with water and a lunch sack with saltines. And do you know what? Nothing ever tasted better than those salty crackers and that cool water from our very own well out there in that dimly lit tent in the middle of the night."

Kimberly closed her eyes, blinking back tears. She knew exactly what Cort was doing, but was powerless to resist. The picture he painted of his childhood was exactly what she wanted for their baby. She went perfectly still, wondering when she'd begun to think of the baby as *theirs*.

"So," he said, after a time. "Did you look at apartments in North Platte today?"

"A few."

"And?"

A hundred thoughts and sensations converged on her mind. She remembered how it had felt to fall asleep in Cort's arms, and how much trouble he'd gone to this past week to get to know her better. She remembered every one of his kisses, and every one of his smiles.

I think you should marry Uncle Cort so your baby won't have to wait until he's seven years old to have a dad. Tommy's words played through her mind like a recorded message. They sent tears to her eyes and a lump to her throat.

Cort didn't know what Kimberly was thinking about, but from the expression on her face, it must have been serious. Moisture swam in her eyes, and even in the darkness, she looked utterly soft, utterly feminine.

A zing went through him, stronger than ever before. Each time it happened, he was amazed by its intensity. This was desire like he'd never known before. It was so hot he could barely control it, so strong he could practically taste it.

He'd taken one look at her at Will and Krista's wedding, and a similar bolt of sexual attraction had come out of nowhere and knocked him on his rear. He wasn't proud of what he'd done, but he wasn't exactly sorry, either. A baby had been conceived that night. A Sutherland. He'd been raised to have high ideals and strong convictions. He and Will had both pushed their limits a little, but it always came back to right or wrong. And marrying Kimberly felt right.

The branches of the cottonwoods sang in the late-night breeze. She glanced up at them, then at him. Their gazes caught, held. And then she smiled.

He couldn't have stopped himself from reaching for her in that instant any more than he could have stopped his next heartbeat. Drawing her closer, he said, "Marry me, Kim. Tonight or tomorrow or next week. You say when. But first, say yes."

Kimberly searched Cort's expression in the moonlight. His eyes looked silver, and held so much promise she barely breathed. She longed to hear words of love on those lips, but simply didn't know how to come out and ask for them.

"Please?"

She heard the earnestness in his softly spoken plea, not to mention the sincerity and the desire, and closed her eyes against the onslaught of emotion filling her every thought.

"Kim?"

"Yes."

"Yes, Cort? Or yes, you'll marry me?"

She opened her eyes. "Yes, Cort. I'll marry you."

His mouth fell open, then spread into a wide smile. "Yee-ha!"

He pulled her to her feet and twirled her around. Kimberly felt like a rag doll, but she'd never been so happy. Maybe he hadn't uttered any words of love, but she had to believe it was there, hovering in the background, slowly making its way to his heart.

He kissed her once, swiftly, happily. "I know we're doing the right thing. Now our baby will have two parents, and the Sutherland name."

Kimberly went still all over again, this time for an entirely different reason. He was doing this for the baby's sake. The baby's. She placed her hand over her abdomen in the exact place their baby was silently growing. She was a little more than two and a half months along, and knew the baby couldn't weigh more than a matter of ounces. But this tiny child already had a tiny little head and eyes and arms and a heart that was already beating with a rhythm all its own.

"You won't be sorry, Kimberly," he said close to her ear. "I promise."

She did her best to tamp down her misgivings, then slowly wavered him a smile through her tears, hoping with everything she had that he was right.

Chapter Five

"She's wearing Grandmother's pearls, so we don't have to worry about finding something old. Now, what about something new?"

"Her dress is new."

"That's true. Now for something borrowed and something blue."

Kimberly dipped a brush into a jar of translucent powder and gently stroked it across her cheeks, wondering when her sisters would realize that she was actually *in* the room. They'd been this way all day, their voices raised in discussion one minute, only to dip into whispered secrets and warm camaraderie the next. They hadn't been this close as children, were in fact only now beginning to appreciate the family ties that bound them. It did her heart good to see it happening before her very eyes. It even helped alleviate her nerves. A little.

"Turn around so we can see you," Katrina instructed.

The moment of truth had arrived. Kimberly swiveled slowly, mentally preparing herself to face the world's toughest critics. Her three sisters—a tax attorney, a college professor and a physical therapist—were all looking her over speculatively just as she knew they would.

Valiantly trying not to feel like a speck beneath a microscope, she looked at each of them in turn and asked, "Did I miss a button, or put my shoes on the wrong feet, or what?"

Three chins jerked up, three pairs of eyes snapping to attention. Katrina, Kendra and Krista glanced at one another and then at her. "Of course not," Katrina, the eldest insisted. "You look beautiful. Although I have to admit I'm a little surprised you decided to wear *pink*. Ow."

Kimberly smiled to herself at the way Katrina rubbed her arm that had just been neatly jabbed by Kendra's sharp elbow. "It's called peach blush, and I think that color looks lovely on her," Kendra admonished.

Kimberly glanced down at herself, her gaze straying over the lace visible above the V-neckline of her jacket, and on down the soft, smooth fabric of her skirt. After leaning ahead slightly in order to see the pointed toes of her matching shoes, she toyed with the pearly buttons on her jacket and asked, "Are you sure this doesn't pull across my chest?"

Krista, who'd always been more endowed in the chest department than the other three Wilson sisters, exchanged a subtle look of amusement with Katrina and Kendra before saying, "It's a perfect fit, and you look positively beautiful. Now would you stop worrying?"

"Stop worrying? You want me to *stop worrying?*"

"Kimberly, you don't *have* to do this," Katrina declared.

If they'd been talking about anything else, Kimberly would have smiled at the way Katrina moved out of range of Kendra's elbow. But this was no laughing matter. She was aware of the gasps her other two sisters took, but she didn't take her eyes from the self-appointed monarch of the group. At thirty-three, Katrina was a noted tax attorney as well as a renowned author of a prizewinning nonfiction book. She was fair like Kimberly and Kendra, but she wore her light blond hair short. Until recently, Kimberly had always thought it matched her personality. Several months ago, she'd started noticing things about her oldest sister she'd never been aware of before. Katrina wasn't as sure of herself as she led them all to believe. Her words might have sounded blunt, but her eyes held genuine affection and, more often than not, worry. It reminded Kimberly that she wasn't the only Wilson whose childhood had been less than ideal.

"Katrina," she said, hearing the softness in her own voice, "I know this seems sudden, but you're the one who insisted I have a real wedding rather than be married by the justice of the peace."

"If you really intend to get married, I think you *should* make it a lasting memory. But there are several alternatives, and even more loopholes. Perfectly safe, perfectly legal, perfectly logical loopholes."

Kimberly glanced at her other two sisters. Kendra may not have voiced her concerns out loud, but the way she was wringing her hands left little doubt that she was worried, too. Turning to Krista, who was listening to the entire conversation with arms crossed and eyes narrowed, Kimberly said, "Do you think I'm doing the wrong thing, too?"

After a drawn-out moment, Krista shook her head. Her wavering smile sent tears to Kimberly's eyes, but it was the feel of her sister's arms gently encircling her shoulders and the long, dark lock of hair tickling her cheek that made her smile through her tears.

"Trust your heart, Kimberly."

Kimberly blinked back tears, once again thinking it was incredible that the one Wilson who hadn't been a child prodigy was the smartest of them all. Looking at her sisters, all of them beautiful in their own right, she said, "I'm glad you could all be here this afternoon. It means a lot to me."

Kendra and Krista both smiled. Surprisingly, Katrina sniffled and said, "We wouldn't have missed it for the world." Pulling herself up to her full height, she squared her shoulders and straightened her navy blue dress. "Now, where were we? Oh, yes. Something borrowed and something blue."

"Oh, my," Kendra said. "The lace handkerchief I tucked in her pocket is blue, but we completely forgot about something borrowed."

"I didn't forget." Krista walked to the closet, reached to a top shelf and brought down a small hat.

Kimberly took it in her hands, smoothing the tip of her fingers across the dainty arch. "Isn't this the hat you wore when you married Will?"

Krista nodded. "It's not only beautiful, it's lucky. My best friend wore it for her wedding three years ago, and loaned it to me. There's something magic about looking at the man you're about to marry through the soft haze of this netting, Kimberly. Here, I'll help you pin it on."

With gentle fingertips, Krista positioned the small hat on the top of Kimberly's head and deftly fastened it, smoothing the net down over her face. "There. You look like a bride already."

There was a commotion on the stairs and a flurry of footsteps in the hall. A glass picture rattled in its frame as Tommy burst into the room. "Mom, Dad says to tell you... wow! Aunt Kimberly, you look really cool."

"He's definitely all male," Kendra declared.

"And all Sutherland," Katrina added.

Kimberly smiled around the lump in her throat. "Thank you, Tommy. Now, what did your dad want you to tell your mom?"

"Oh, yeah," he answered impishly. "The reverend is ready when you are."

Kimberly turned back to the mirror for one final inspection. Kendra joined her, saying, "I think you have everything, don't you? Something old, something new, something borrowed and something blue."

"Tell your dad we're on our way," Krista told her son.

The picture frame rattled again as Tommy clomped down the stairs. Seconds later, strains of guitar music floated into the spare bedroom where Kimberly had been staying these past two weeks.

Kendra ruffled the edge of her beige suit. "I guess that's our cue."

"Yes, I guess it is," Kimberly whispered.

The four sisters looked at one another, then started to move toward the door. "Kimberly, wait!" Katrina whispered.

Searching Katrina's expression, Kimberly asked, "What is it?"

"Before we all go downstairs, there's one thing I have to ask. If I don't, and things don't work out, I'll never forgive myself."

"Okay, Katrina. Go ahead."

"Are you sure you're not marrying Cort simply because you *have* to?"

Looking at all the family she had in the world, Kimberly shook her head. "I'm not sure about everything, Katrina, but I know there's a lot more to this than that. I'm marrying Cort because I want to. I love him. And I think I'm going to take Krista's advice and trust my heart."

Krista gave her a warm wink, and, one by one, the sisters lined up. Kimberly followed them down the open staircase. Krista, Kendra and Katrina took their places along the side of the room, leaving Kimberly standing alone on the bottom step. She was aware of several pairs of eyes on her—her sisters', of course, and Tommy's. Will and Joe and Evelyn Sutherland were looking at her, too, as was Reverend Jones and his wife, who was playing the guitar. Nerves clamored through Kimberly, her eyes automatically moving toward the front of the room.

She wasn't aware of the small smile of enchantment touching her lips. She was only aware of the man looking at her from across the room. There wasn't much of the cowboy left in Cort today. His dark suit and tie fit his body perfectly, his white shirt making his skin appear even darker than normal. His hair looked freshly cut, his gaze unwavering.

Her breath caught in her throat, aching just a little. Krista had been right. There was something magical about gazing at the man she was about to marry through the hazy net of a wedding hat.

Her heart pounded an erratic rhythm as she descended the last step. Raising her chin ever so slightly, Kendra's rhyme echoed through her mind. Something old, something new, something borrowed, something blue. Taking one step, and then another and another, she said a silent prayer for the most important thing of all. Cort's love.

Cort turned so that he could face Kimberly across the expanse of his brother's living room. He heard the soft chords of the wedding song coming from Gretta's guitar, not to mention the gasps and murmurs from the few people present for today's big event. Not more than ten seconds ago, he'd been pulling at the starched collar of his shirt. Suddenly, everything faded—the music, his family, his discomfort—everything except the sight of Kimberly slowly walking toward him.

He took the few remaining steps to meet her and offered her his arm. She hesitated for a moment, and he held his breath.

For crying out loud, he'd been like this all week, his pulse speeding up one minute, slowing to a crawl the next, never completely sure that Kimberly wouldn't change her mind at any given moment. He'd done everything but beg her not to go back to Boston to pack up her things, certain that if she saw the life she was leaving behind, she'd never come back to Nebraska. Surprisingly, she'd arrived back yesterday. But he wouldn't breathe easy until Reverend Jones pronounced them husband and wife.

She looked up at him, the top half of her face slightly obscured behind a delicate white net attached to her hat. Her blue, blue eyes delved his. Her expression softened, and she smiled. His breath caught in his chest as if he'd been kicked in the gut.

At long last, she placed her hand in the crook of his elbow and looked at him expectantly. Another sensation took hold of his body, this one far more enjoyable than the last. For the first time all week, he felt his old loftiness kick in. He puffed up his chest and covered her hand with his, proudly leading her to the front of the room.

"Dearly beloved. We are gathered here today to join Cort Joseph Sutherland and Kimberly Susannah Wilson in marriage."

The reverend continued to read from his frayed book. Cort answered when appropriate, but he was barely aware of the actual words. His heart pumped in his chest, his thoughts taking him down a shadowy path in his imagination where words weren't necessary.

"Do you, Kimberly Susannah Wilson, take this man to be your lawfully wedded husband?"

The room had grown completely silent. Even the wind outside had grown quiet, waiting. Cort forced himself to breathe, his eyes holding hers. And then, in a voice so soft he had to strain to hear, she said, "I do."

He wanted to swing her off her feet then and there, but managed to hold on to his composure long enough for the reverend to say, "Do you, Cort Joseph Sutherland, take this woman to be your lawfully wedded wife?"

"I sure do."

There were murmurs and quiet laughter behind him, but Cort's gaze was riveted on Kim's face.

"I now pronounce you husband and wife. Cort, you may kiss your bride."

"I've been waiting all day to hear you say that," Cort proclaimed.

This time the guests laughed outright. Cort paid them no attention. He drew Kimberly closer. And kissed his wife.

"Well, it looks like you convinced her," Cort's father said with a spry wink. "Always knew you could do it."

Cort heard the out-and-out jauntiness in his father's voice. Glancing sideways, he saw the way his mother rolled her eyes. But he was too busy watching Kimberly's every move to pay his parents much attention.

Things had gone pretty darned good, if he did say so himself. Even Katrina's long-eyed stare couldn't chase away his inner excitement tonight. The tiny reception Will and Krista had hosted in his and Kimberly's honor was nearly over. Any minute now, the newlyweds would be able to leave. Cort could hardly wait.

Kimberly looked at him from across the room, the soft lamplight threading the pale blond tendrils loosely secured on her head with deeper colors of wheat and golden honey. She held her shoulders regally, the material of her jacket following her smooth contours the way he wanted to. Only he wouldn't be content to leave her covered. Oh, no, he'd slip those buttons loose and gently glide the fabric over her shoulders and down her arms. He wouldn't stop there. Oh, no, he wouldn't stop until they were husband and wife in every way. His fantasies sent an ache all the way through him, thrumming, pulsing, waiting.

"See, Evvie? After all these years, you're getting the large family I promised you. Two sons, one grandchild and another on the way. And girls, Evvie. Finally, we're getting the girls, in the form of daughters-in-law, and maybe even a granddaughter or two, you always dreamed of."

Cort's heart beat a steady rhythm in his chest, his body taut and heavy, his desire under control, but just barely. Through the roaring din in his ears, he heard his father's words, and in some far-off corner of his mind, a memory, too vague and shadowy for clear recollection, hovered.

Evelyn Sutherland smiled at her second-born. "Don't let your father's softheartedness fool you. He's just happy because of the rain."

"See that?" Joe sputtered, a smile not far from his lips. "I try to be sentimental, and she brings up the weather. Honestly, it's all this woman ever thinks about."

They kissed, these two people who had raised him. For an instant, his mother appeared as breathless as a schoolgirl, but her eyes danced knowingly, and a woman's smile played across her mouth. Suddenly, Cort had an inkling of how his father saw his mother. Evelyn—Evvie, as his father called her—was on the tall side for a woman; her short dark hair was threaded with gray. Her eyes were crinkled at the corners from all her years of peering out over the Nebraska landscape. He supposed she'd always been attractive, but there was something about her, an inner light that made a person stand up and take notice.

She laughed just as she had nearly every day he'd known her. Except for that one summer when he was seven. A memory hovered on the edge of his mind. He tried to bring it into focus, but across the room, Kimberly leaned down and hugged Tommy, her eyes meeting his over the little boy's dark head. Cort lost his train of thought completely.

"Go ahead," Evelyn said, placing her hand on her grown son's shoulder. "I know you're aching to take your new bride home."

He kissed his mother's cheek, surprising them both, then straightened. "Thanks for the advice, Mom. I think I'll do that."

Turning on his heel, he strode to Kimberly's side.

The truck's back tire splashed through another pothole, the headlights illuminating the pelting rain. The weather was one reason Cort was glad he didn't have far to drive. But it wasn't the most important reason, not by a long shot.

"Are you warm enough?" he asked.

"Yes, I'm fine."

Kimberly's voice had come from the other side of the truck where she was huddled close to the door. Keeping both hands on the wheel and his eyes on the shallow washout up ahead, he said, "You can change the radio station if you want to."

"This one's fine."

That was the third time she'd used the word *fine*, and they'd only gone two miles. He'd apologized for the rust on the outside of his truck, for the rattles on the inside and for the static on the radio. Hell, he'd even apologize for the rain if he thought it would help put her at ease. He'd stand on his head if it would make her slide closer and maybe put her hand on his knee. There wasn't much he *wouldn't* do to have her slide her hand up his thigh.

Thoughts like those carried him over the next three miles. He pulled into his driveway, certain the ride had never taken longer. Shutting off the engine, he peered through the wet windshield and said, "I forgot to bring an umbrella."

"Yes. So did I."

"Here," he said, moving to shrug out of his suit jacket. "At least put this over your dress."

"A little rain isn't going to hurt me, Cort. I won't melt, you know."

Even with her face turned toward the window, he heard the authority in her voice. Man, he loved it when she turned all haughty and indignant. He toyed with the idea of reaching for her blindly and kissing her. But in his condition, he wasn't sure he'd be able to stop, and he wanted tonight to be as close to perfect as anything had ever been.

"Come on," she said. "We're going to have to make a run for it."

The handle clicked, the door creaked and the dome light burst on. "On the count of three," she declared. "One. Two. Three."

Cort shrugged back into his coat and pushed open his own door, grabbing her suitcase from the back of the truck. Even with their mad dash, they were both soaking wet by the time they made it to the small side porch. But now, they were both smiling, too.

He opened the door and flicked on the light, then followed her inside. After kicking the door shut, he set the suitcase on the worn linoleum and moved to take her in his arms. She spun out of his reach so quickly his fingers came into contact with nothing but air.

"Kimberly," he said, following much more slowly. "There's no need to be nervous."

"Who said I was nervous?"

Cocking one eyebrow, he evaluated the situation. She was standing on one side of the rectangular-shaped table, he on the other. She'd removed her hat earlier, not that it would have been much protection against the pouring rain. The deluge of water had dampened her hair, sending several tendrils trailing from the intricate twist on her head. She dried her hands on her skirt, then hid them behind her back and fastened her gaze somewhere in the vicinity of his chin.

If she wasn't nervous, he'd eat his favorite hat.

"You're probably cold in that wet dress," he said, letting his hands fall to the back of a kitchen chair.

"I'm fine."

That was her fourth *fine* in ten minutes. But who was counting?

He followed the course of her gaze around his kitchen. The Sutherlands had bought this spread ten years ago from an old couple whose health had forced them to move into town. They'd left most of their furniture behind. Looking at the old metal table, he realized what a relic from the sixties it was. It was a dull gray color with a worn Formica top. It had always served its purpose, holding a plate and fork perfectly. It was easy to wash, too. Now, he wished he'd have taken the time to replace it with something more modern.

He wanted to loosen the knot of his tie, but didn't think it would be wise to begin undressing just yet. Keeping his voice soft and deep, he said, "I guess this house doesn't look like much, does it?"

Her eyes flew to his and opened wide. "Are you kidding? People in the city are paying a fortune for these tables and chairs. They're so retro."

Cort wasn't sure what that meant, but it couldn't have been too bad. She was smiling, after all.

"If you like it, you can leave it. But feel free to change anything in the entire house. This *is* your home now."

"Yes, I suppose you're right."

"Now," he said, his voice taking on a new huskiness. "Why don't you come here so I can kiss you properly?"

She gulped, her throat convulsing so much he saw it from his side of the table. "Could we talk a little? First, I mean?"

Something went warm inside Cort, something far deeper than his wet clothes and outer layers of skin. "Okay," he said, taking a step closer. "But why don't we go into the living room where it's warmer and more comfortable?"

He waited until she'd rounded the table, then slowly offered her his hand. She placed her fingers in his, and he led her into the next room where he settled his long frame onto the old couch. She lowered to a cushion a short distance from him, then glanced at him shyly. "You're going to think I'm a complete dimwit, but I can't seem to think of a thing to say."

Cort took his time loosening his tie, then rested his arm on the back of the couch where his fingers toyed with her hair. "Why don't you tell me how a woman as beautiful and intelligent as you made it all the way to her thirtieth birthday a virgin?"

Kimberly jerked her head around, her eyes meeting his. The tenderness in his expression amazed her. It sent a shock through her, but it also warmed her from the inside much the way the fingers gliding through the hair at her nape warmed her neck.

After a moment of careful deliberation during which she tried to decide where to begin, she said, "I don't know how much Krista has told you about our childhood."

"She's told me next to nothing, and I'm glad. I'd rather hear about it from you."

Kimberly felt her eyelashes flutter down. As usual, the man was wreaking havoc with her senses. Settling her gaze on the faded wallpaper across the room, she said, "My sisters and I are all close in age, but until recently, we haven't been close in any other way. Looking back, I don't think it was anybody's fault. My mother died a few years ago, but my father passed away when we were all very young. He left my mother with a good-size insurance policy, and four daughters to raise on her own. She did her best, but I think we were more than she could handle. I started talking when I was one. Katrina and Kendra were even younger. Mother took us to experts, and followed their advice. Consequently, we spent most of our childhood living in boarding schools for gifted children."

"All-girl boarding schools?"

She nodded. "Honestly, I never even kissed a boy until I was seventeen. It happened during a joint study session between the boys' boarding school and mine. Robert was sixteen, and had an IQ that rivaled Einstein's. He was tall and thin and serious, with a shock of dark hair that refused to lie down in the front. Anyway, one day I looked up from my notebook and found him watching me. He told me point-blank that he'd like to kiss me. So, we both stood, and it happened. Afterward, he went back to his charts and logarithms, and I went back to calculus."

"He never kissed you again?"

"No."

"That's a shame, Kim, because I don't believe I've ever seen a pair of lips more kissable than yours."

Kimberly turned her head and found herself staring into the darkest blue eyes she'd ever seen. Goose bumps skittered down her arms, but far deeper, she felt inordinately warmed.

"I'm not complaining about the fact that you were a virgin that night, Kimberly. What you gave me was a rare gift."

She watched his lips move, the sound of his words like secrets whispered in the dark of night. His shirt was open at the neck, his tie loose and crooked. His eyelashes dipped down now and then, but his lazy, hazy gaze never left her face.

When she'd first told him about the baby two weeks ago, she'd insisted that she didn't expect anything from him. Now, she was his wife. She'd vowed to win his love. Staring at his rugged features, she saw infinite tenderness, and incredible desire. But she couldn't be sure there was love.

Trust your heart. Those had been Krista's only words of advice.

Kimberly searched her mind for what she should say, but she searched her heart for what she should do. And in her heart, she found love for this man.

Trusting her heart, she raised her face toward his and whispered, "I've learned a few things about kissing since Robert. If you'd like, I could show you right now."

He smiled that roguish smile that melted her knees and turned her heart to mush. "I wasn't the best student in school, Kimberly. But when it comes to kissing, I'm more than willing to learn anything you'd like to teach me."

She leaned ahead, letting her lips skim his. Gaining confidence, she parted them, and the kiss deepened. The hand that had been caressing her nape moved down her back, drawing her closer to the length of his torso. Her hands spread wide across his chest, kneading his warm flesh, then slowly moving around to the back of his shoulders.

She'd never realized how challenging, and rewarding, kissing a man could be. His mouth was firm where hers was soft, his breathing deep where hers was shallow. But their sighs were equally deep throated, and their need, equally strong.

He cupped her face in one large hand, then splayed his fingers wide through her hair, uncaring that it loosened clasps and brought her hair tumbling around her shoulders in wild disarray. She changed the angle of her mouth over his and tentatively smoothed her tongue along his lower lip.

He groaned deep in his throat, and with the speed and strength of a cyclone, he found his feet, bringing her up with him. Everything blurred after that. She was vaguely aware of doorways, of her feet moving across the floor, and of rain hitting windowpanes along the way. But she didn't really surface until she was in a bedroom lit only by the light from the hall.

"Kimberly."

His voice was little more than a rasp in the darkness, but his hands made his intentions vibrantly clear. They skimmed her shoulders, then glided down to her waist, only to find their way back up again where he made short work of releasing the five buttons down the center. He pushed her jacket from her shoulders, and she pulled her arms from the sleeves. Seconds later, the fabric made a quiet swish as it landed on the floor.

The air felt damp and dusky, like it might in a jungle in some long-lost fairy tale. But the sound of Cort's breathing wasn't fantasy, nor was the heat of his touch. He was real, and he was here, and he was her husband.

The realization spurred her movements and banished her shyness. She pulled his tie from his neck, then deftly unfastened every button down his shirt. So impatient to be rid of his clothes, he tried to pull the shirt from his arms, only to get it stuck over his hands where the buttons at his cuffs were still fastened.

"Patience, Cort," she whispered on a deep laugh. "We have all night."

Cort tossed the shirt aside after she undid the buttons, then glided his arms around her. She wanted him to be patient? He thought about telling her patience had never been his strong suit, but decided to show her instead.

He'd spent a good deal of time wondering what she was wearing underneath her dress today. Now, he barely gave the soft, silky garments a moment's notice. He pushed her skirt down her hips, helped her out of her shoes, then whisked her slip and other scraps of lace away.

She stood before him, naked. Beautiful. Quivering.

His desire was so strong he couldn't get out of his remaining clothes fast enough. One of his shoes hit the wall behind him, his pants ending up in an inside-out heap at his feet. He had no idea where his briefs landed, but he didn't care. All he cared about was kissing her again, and drawing her with him toward the bed, urging her hands to explore him the way she had their first night together.

It had been nearly three months since that night. Three long, lonely months. Although he preferred not to admit it out loud, he'd gone longer than that without sex, lots of times. But three months had never seemed like three years, and he'd never felt such a burning need to make a woman his. Until now.

They fell to the bed, their arms and legs tangled. She laughed softly, and he caught the sound in his next kiss. She kneaded his back, starting at his shoulders and slowly, surely, working her way down. His entire back tingled at her touch as wave after wave of hungry desire spiraled through him.

His lips left hers to trail kisses along her jaw, down the smooth column of her neck and on down to the soft peaks of her breasts. He took them both in his hands, loving her soft moan, loving the way they swelled at his touch, filling his palms in a way he didn't remember.

She might have had her shy moments in the light of day, but in bed, she was brazen and needy and damned incredible. As if she was unwilling to let him be the only one to bring them pleasure, she let her hands trail down his body, sighing when she found what she'd been searching for.

Cort groaned out loud. Rolling her onto her back, he skimmed her waist with his hands, then brought them together low on her abdomen. Her stomach had been flat three months ago. Now it was slightly rounded, not enough to notice in her clothes, but out of them, now that was a different story. He smiled as he planted a kiss in the very center.

And then he went very still.

Chapter Six

The wind blew through the dark night, rattling a shutter and scraping a branch against the wet siding as if it had nothing better to do. It was long past the bewitching hour, and Kimberly knew she should try to sleep. But she couldn't.

Being careful not to jostle the extrafirm bed, she turned over onto her back and closed her eyes. They sprang open again, just as they had every other time she'd attempted to shut them since she and Cort had made love.

The rain had stopped an hour ago. She couldn't say the same for her thoughts. Staring up at the dark ceiling, she'd relived everything that had happened after she'd kissed Cort on his living room sofa.

At first, their lovemaking had been incredible, his lips so coaxing, his hands so demanding, she'd been about to go up like a match on dry tinder. But then, something changed. Oh, it had still been enjoyable, but his movements had become less frenzied, more careful, more controlled.

He'd kissed her tenderly when it was all over, and had stroked her hair when she'd curled up close. She'd fully expected him to reach for her again, as he had their first night together. Instead, the hand stroking her hair had gradually stilled, his breathing growing deep and steady.

Feeling strangely lost and abandoned, she'd inched her way to her own side of the bed where she'd gone over and over the entire evening in her mind, from the moment she'd said, "I do," to the moment Cort drifted off to sleep. She remembered how nervous she'd been during the ride here. But his roguish smile was all it had taken to put her at ease, and to warm her from the inside out. She'd loved kissing him, and had reveled in the way he'd responded to her touch. He'd levered himself over her, working magic every place he touched. He'd kissed her in places that would have made her blush in the light of day, even pressing his lips to her stomach where their child was growing.

She smoothed her hand over her abdomen, her mind beginning to drift. Cort had been putting in long hours that stretched beyond sunup to sundown, and he'd made time to see her, as well. The poor man was probably tired to the bone. Snuggling into her pillow, she reminded herself that she really had no reason to complain. He *had* been wonderful tonight, so caring and tender and concerned with her needs. By tomorrow, he'd be rested and back to his old self again. Who knew? By then, he might even begin to fall in love with her.

He made a sound in his sleep. Kimberly smiled into the darkness, her eyelashes fluttering down. The mattress seemed to curl up around her body, the sounds of night coming from farther and farther away. She heard a sigh that might have been hers and smiled again. Carrying her smile into sleep with her, she dreamed of firm lips nuzzling hers, and strong arms wrapping her in passion, and, ultimately, in love.

Kimberly's body felt so warm and languid she might have been floating. Half sighing and half humming, she moved her head slightly to give the lips nuzzling her neck better access, smiling when they found a ticklish spot. She moaned softly, amazed at how real her dream seemed. Those lips trailed up her neck, brushing a kiss along her jaw, smoothing over her cheek, inching closer to her mouth. The bed creaked slightly, and she moved automatically toward the slight decline where she came into contact with a firm hip and thigh.

Her dream didn't make sense. Why would Cort's thigh be covered with denim? Before she could force herself awake, his lips covered hers, and she gave up trying to think. Twining her hands around broad shoulders, she heard the bed creak again, followed by a softly murmured moan, neither of which came from her.

She opened her eyes slowly, and realization dawned. The eyes staring into hers were dreamy, but they weren't a figment of her imagination. They were as real as Cort himself, as real as the heat in his gaze and the answering warmth deep inside her.

"Good morning," she whispered, wondering where the note of shyness in her voice had come from.

Cort lifted his face from hers. "Mornin'. You were sleeping so peacefully I almost didn't bother you, but I didn't want you to wake up alone later and wonder where I'd gone."

She let his words soak through her sleepy haze. It was still dark outside, but it must have been close to dawn, because the air was more gray than black. Now that her eyes had adjusted, she could see that he was wearing jeans and a denim shirt.

"Cort?"

"Hmm?"

"What would you say if I told you that you aren't bothering me in the least?"

She thought she heard him groan, but he was off the bed and across the room so fast she couldn't be sure she hadn't imagined it.

"You need your rest," he said from the doorway.

She propped herself up on her elbows, the sheet slowly inching lower. Kimberly felt his eyes on her in the semi-darkness, and fought the inclination to pull the blankets up around her neck. She was a married woman now, a married woman who wanted her husband to crawl back into bed with her.

She could hear his deeply drawn breath from here. Although she couldn't see his expression, his body language spoke volumes. He was fidgety, and as jumpy as a cat on hot bricks.

"Don't you? Need your rest, I mean," she asked.

"I'm used to living on a few hours a night. Go back to sleep and I'll see you later," he said, his voice a little gruff, a little husky.

"Where are you going?"

"Frank and Mo have the weekend off, so I have to help Pokey feed cattle."

"How long do you think you'll be gone?"

The floorboards creaked beneath his boots as he shifted from one foot to the other. "A couple of hours, at least."

"Oh. Well. If you have to go, I guess you have to go."

He shifted his weight again before saying, "Yeah. I guess you're right."

The bed was underneath the window, the white sheets seemingly surrounded by a vaguely sensuous light. Kimberly arched her back, moving with all the provocative grace and pure feminine wile she possessed. She could feel the intensity of his gaze, but not a single floorboard creaked. She hoped it was because he was in the process of changing his mind about leaving and was about to climb back into bed with her.

"Is something wrong?" she asked quietly.

His chin jerked up several inches in the gathering light of dawn. "What could possibly be wrong?"

His voice sounded hoarse. Kimberly smiled.

"I can't think of a thing," she answered, stretching like a cat in a patch of sunshine.

He cleared his throat. "I'll see you when I get back."

"I'm looking forward to it, Cort. I truly am."

He made enough noise for ten men as he marched down the short hall, tramped through the kitchen and hiked out the back door. She snuggled down under the covers, letting her anticipation carry her thoughts away.

She knew she was no expert on men. That was quite possibly the world's largest understatement. But she remembered an old saying one of her housemothers used to spout. *The way to a man's heart is through his stomach.* Sometime between the last kiss Cort had given her last night and the one that had awakened her this morning, she'd had a startling revelation. The way to Cort's heart could very well be via the bed.

She reached for his pillow. It was firm and large, like he was. Wrapping both arms around it, she inhaled the mingled scents of his after-shave, shampoo and the man himself. With anticipation slowing her thoughts, she whispered, "If the way to his heart really is via the bed, maybe he was right. Maybe I do need my rest."

She turned onto her side, taking Cort's pillow with her. And closed her eyes once again.

Cort grabbed the last bale of hay and heaved it over the side of his truck. Placing one gloved hand on the tailgate, he vaulted to the ground.

He'd cut the twine on half the bales by the time Pokey rumbled to a stop in his battered old Jeep. Damn. Cort had hoped to finish the entire job before anyone else showed up.

"What are *you* doin' here?" Pokey groused, his voice more gravelly than usual at this early hour.

"I'm feeding these cattle. What does it look like I'm doing?"

Cort didn't like the narrow-eyed stare he was getting from his best cowhand, and applied about ten times more pressure than was necessary to the knife, nearly splitting the bale in two. He swore under his breath and tossed more hay over the fence where a small herd of Herefords were already chewing lazily.

"Well, don't that beat all?"

"Doesn't what beat all?" Cort sputtered, shooing a curious heifer away with his hat.

"You bein' here this morning, that's what."

Eyeing the next bale, Cort said, "I knew Mo and Frank were off this weekend, and since you aren't as young as you used to be, I decided to get the job done myself."

Pokey Pierson hooked his thumbs beneath his suspenders and literally glared at Cort. "I've been feedin' cattle nearly every day of my sixty-odd years. The day I'm too old to do it is the day you might as well put me six feet under."

He stopped suddenly and scratched at his scraggly, whiskery beard. "Well, I'll be goldarned. I knew I should have taken you aside and given you a little advice before the weddin', but you were running 'round here like a chicken with its head off all week long and I just couldn't catch you. B'sides, I thought you knew what you was doin'."

"I did know what I was doing!" Cort slammed his hat back on his head and scowled. He'd fallen right into that one.

"Then things went all right 'tween you and the new missus?"

Cort cut through the last piece of twine, the bale of hay immediately sagging around the edges. "Of course *things* went all right. Now, are you going to stand around here watching me work? Or are you going to get busy yourself?"

Pokey reared up indignantly and turned on his skinny bowed legs. Cort couldn't quite make out everything the old man said, but he caught the gist of his grumblings.

"...to come right out and tell me I'm gittin' old...I oughta...b'sides, it seems mighty strange that a man who just spent the night with his new bride would wake up ornerier than a pet snake."

Cort fought the urge to yell, "It takes one to know one," then finished feeding the herd by himself, which suited him to a T. It gave him time to think, time to evaluate the situation and time to plan what to do about it.

He hadn't been lying when he'd told Pokey that *things* had gone all right. Damn, they'd started out a helluva lot better than that. He'd been as ready as he could get long before the reverend gave him permission to kiss his bride. And when Kimberly had removed his tie and deftly unbuttoned his shirt, he'd nearly come apart at the seams. Just like the first night they were together, their sighs had been throaty, their breathing ragged, their wants and needs as lusty as they could possibly be.

Kimberly had been ardent and passionate and so damned willing he was getting worked up again just thinking about it. He'd planned to make her so glad she'd married him she'd never want to leave. The strange thing was, the more pleasure he brought her, the greater his own need became. She'd writhed beneath him, and he'd nearly used up the last of his restraint. Then his hands had glided to her stomach. In his state, it was amazing he'd noticed the difference in her body. But placing his hands over the exact place where their child was growing, the memory of his mother's tears and his father's ashen face had flashed through his mind.

For crying out loud, no man wants to think about his parents at a time like that. But something his father had said at the reception, along with the slight rounding of Kim's belly had jarred his memory to the summer when he was seven, the summer his mother lost her smile and his father blamed himself.

Cort had never been a man who took responsibility lightly. The fact that he hadn't used protection with Kimberly nearly three months ago was difficult enough to swallow. He wasn't proud of it, but he'd done the right thing and married her. He knew he hadn't exactly been gentle with her the first time they made love, or the second, for that matter. But by God, he wasn't going to do anything that might harm her or the baby now.

That wasn't going to be easy, because he had a hard time thinking straight when she was in his arms. Hell, he had a hard time thinking straight when she was in the same room. In fact, he hadn't had it this bad since he'd first figured out what the hormones charging through his body meant.

Cort folded his knife, then pulled his glove off with his teeth. Looking out over his ranch, he reminded himself that he wasn't a kid anymore. He was a thirty-year-old man, and he was going to be a father. He knew firsthand the kinds of sacrifices his own father had made for his family. Joe Sutherland had been a good teacher. Luckily, Cort had paid attention.

He took off his other glove, then strode around to the driver's side of the truck and climbed in. The engine chugged to life, the tires kicking up mud as he found first gear and headed for the house where his pregnant wife was waiting.

Kimberly munched on a saltine cracker and meandered from one room to the next. Cort had said he'd be gone two hours, at least. So far, he'd been gone two and a half.

Passing a mirror, she surveyed her reflection. She'd slept another hour after Cort left, then took a long, refreshing shower. Maybe it was the country water, but she didn't think her hair had ever looked so clean and healthy. It had a tendency to wave when she let it air-dry. This morning it reached past her shoulders, the tendrils soft looking and shiny and the tiniest bit unruly. It was a different look for her, but she liked it. The question was, would Cort?

She'd stood at the foot of the bed, peering into her suitcase for a long time, trying to decide what to wear to carry out her plan. She once saw a segment on a TV talk show about a woman who greeted her husband at the door wearing nothing but plastic wrap and a smile. Kimberly had always been a cover-up kind of woman. Her swimsuits had always been one piece, and she didn't even own a teddy or a garter belt, for heaven's sake. Plastic wrap was definitely out of the question. Most of her things were en route from Boston, so the best she could do this morning was a knee-length satin robe in powder blue. She didn't know if it looked sexy, but...

Footsteps sounded on the back porch. Kimberly froze for a moment. Girded by her resolve, she forced herself to saunter into the kitchen as casual as could be. She didn't cross her arms, and she didn't fidget. She just moseyed around the table, tipped her head ever so slightly to one side and said, "You're back."

Cort turned at the sound of her voice, his hand falling away from his hat, which he'd hung on a peg near the door. "Yeah, I guess I am."

"I'm glad," she said, smiling softly.

His eyes narrowed, his throat convulsing on a swallow. "I thought you might still be sleeping."

"I've been up for a while. Actually, I've had a marvelous morning. But I've been looking forward to you getting back."

If she was a person who could have seen auras, she'd bet his just changed color. His throat convulsed again, and he raked his fingers through his hair.

"Have you had breakfast?" he asked.

"A bowl of cereal. And my usual dose of saltines. Have you?"

"Not yet. I'm sorry about this, Kimberly. I thought we could go into North Platte and have breakfast together. What kind of a honeymoon is it when the bride has to eat her first breakfast as a married woman alone?"

Kimberly sashayed closer. "I understand, Cort. Our wedding happened so fast neither one of us has had a lot of time to plan."

"We'll take a real honeymoon later, I promise."

Her mouth curved into an unconscious smile as she said, "I've always thought of a honeymoon as a time rather than a place. How about you?"

He took the few remaining steps separating them. Splaying his fingers through her hair, he breathed a kiss on her mouth. Her body heated and her muscles seemed to melt. She expected him to take her into his arms and kiss her more thoroughly. Instead, he raised his face from hers and strode a few feet toward the door.

"Still," he said, his voice unusually hoarse. "I intend to give you a proper honeymoon later."

"I'd like that, Cort. In the meantime, I want to be a true partner in your life."

Before her eyes, his face brightened, and a look she could only call relief found its way to his features. "Do you mean that?"

"Absolutely."

"All right, then. Let's go." He reached for his hat with one hand and for her fingers with the other.

Kimberly took the few steps separating them and placed her hand in his, her confidence spiraling. She'd been worried that he wouldn't accept her into his life, into his heart. Feeling elated, her thoughts spun to what lay ahead.

But he didn't move.

And neither did she.

What was he waiting for, and why was he wearing his hat?

"I'll just grab a few slices of toast while you get ready."

His simple statement caught her off guard. "I beg your pardon?"

"You said you wanted to be a true partner in my life."

"I do."

"Good. Then don't you think you'd better get dressed?"

Kimberly felt her mouth drop open, her astonishment rendering her momentarily speechless. "Get dressed?" she finally managed to whisper.

For a genius, she must have sounded like an idiot.

"Jeans and a T-shirt would probably be more comfortable than your nightgown, at least on the range. Oh, you'd better wear boots, too, because the ground's muddy after last night's rain. I'll pack a lunch while you're getting ready. We could be out all day."

She stared at him for a full five seconds. Seeing the range was definitely not how she'd planned to spend the remainder of her morning, but the look on Cort's face and the set of his chin left little room for argument.

Clamping her mouth shut, she spun around and headed for the bedroom, thinking that maybe she should have tried the plastic wrap, after all.

"Okay, now let me get this straight," Kimberly said, squinting into the sun. "A group of cattle is called a herd, and a herd consists of cows, bulls, steers, heifers and calves."

"You're a fast learner."

Glancing up at Cort's profile, she said, "It's a gift. Or a hindrance, depending upon your perspective."

Instead of using any of the trite lines she'd heard a million times before, he shrugged in an offhand manner and pointed to a small group of cattle on the horizon. "We try to keep the cattle together this time of the year. During the winter, they break apart into smaller herds to find food. Come spring, a few of them always get rangy. If there's a sinkhole within a ten-mile radius, I can guarantee that at least one of them will find it."

Kimberly didn't have to pretend to be interested in every word he said. The workings of the ranch were fascinating. Not as fascinating as what she'd *planned* to spend her morning doing, but fascinating in their own way.

"Okay," she said when he paused to take a breath. "A cow is a female and a bull is a male. Calves are babies, of course, and a young cow is called a heifer until she gives birth. Oh, and last but not least, steers are males whose reproductive organs have been removed. Poor things. And none of them, not cows, bulls, calves, steers or heifers, have names."

Cort came to a sudden stop. He stayed where he was, waiting for her to notice that she was walking alone. It didn't take her long to glance over her shoulder. "What is it, Cort? You look a little surprised."

He was surprised all right, surprised as hell, but not that she remembered everything he'd told her. What surprised him was her attitude, her insuppressible thirst for knowledge, her inquisitiveness and her subtle humor.

They'd been out here on the range for hours, and she showed no signs of tiring. He'd pointed out the different types of cattle they herded, giving her a brief overview of their attributes and problems. She didn't comment that branding cattle was inhumane. She *did* look a little green around the gills when he mentioned castrating the bull calves, but he could hardly blame her. He always cringed a little, himself, at the thought of that one.

If she didn't understand something, she asked questions, some simple, some not, her mind soaking up information the way the Sand Hills soaked up rain. But she wasn't all questions. If she had an opinion, she voiced it. For instance, she told him in no uncertain terms that applying lye to the "little dickens'" horns was downright cruel. And she never missed an opportunity to point out that cattle deserved names just like everyone else.

"Are you going to stand there all day?"

Cort felt his eyebrows go up at the challenge in her voice. The woman-soft smile she wavered at him was having a similar effect on an entirely different part of his body. Kimberly Wilson—Kimberly *Sutherland*, now—was damn near impossible to resist.

He took a deep breath and blew it all out. Settling his hat lower on his forehead, he took another, calling up his inner strength and all the good old Sutherland pluck it was going to take to hold his ground and withstand her charms.

"Well?" she asked. "*Are* you coming?"

"At this rate, you're going to see the entire two thousand acres in one day."

Kimberly watched him walk toward her. From the back, his loose-jointed stroll would have been called a swagger. She wasn't sure what to call it from the front, but he looked every bit as good walking toward her as he looked walking away. Maybe better.

"Then you're surprised by my stamina?"

She couldn't help noticing the way his eyes dropped down at her double entendre. She couldn't help noticing the fit of his jeans, either. He wanted her. Somehow, she hoped to turn that *want* into love.

"How about that lunch I promised you?" he asked, his voice a little huskier than it had been a few minutes ago.

Her stomach rumbled at the mention of food, and she laughed, saying, "I thought you'd never ask."

They ate their picnic lunch sitting on a fence somewhere in the middle of the Sutherland ranch. Afterward, they climbed back into the four-wheel-drive Jeep she'd seen the ranch hands use and headed west. They hadn't gone far when he stopped suddenly and jumped out.

"Where are you going?" she asked.

"It's a secret, but don't move. I'll be right back."

True to his word, he came back a few minutes later, a small bouquet of the first violets of the season in his callused hand. Kimberly accepted the flowers. Inhaling their delicate scent, she thought her heart might just melt and slide all the way down to her stomach.

They didn't say much for the next half hour. The silence was companionable, and gave Kimberly some time with her thoughts. Cort Sutherland was a caring man, there was no doubt about that. And one of these days, he was going to realize that he was falling in love with her, she just knew it.

Pointing to a series of hills rising in the north, she said, "I didn't know Nebraska was so hilly."

"Those are the Sand Hills. They cover more than twenty thousand square miles of this section of Nebraska and consist of sand piled into hills and ridges by the wind. Some of the best grazing grasses in the west cover the hills, holding most of the sand in place."

They drove on in silence until they came to what looked like a large crater. "What in the world happened there?" she asked.

"That's called a blowout," he said. "It happened years before we bought the land and was caused by overgrazing. Once the grass was gone, the wind cut this huge hole into the hill. Ranchers in these parts have to be extra careful not to let that happen."

Kimberly was in awe of the vastness of the land, and of the harsh elements Cort and every other rancher in these parts dealt with every day of their lives. There was something about it that left her feeling invigorated, challenged, excited.

After an hour, he turned around and headed southeast. They ate their dinner—or supper, as Cort called it—in a small diner in North Platte. Cort didn't say anything when she ordered fish and a salad instead of red meat, but she thought she detected a knowing little glint in his eyes as he dug into his own thick steak.

Pleasantly full and pleasingly relaxed following all the walking they'd done, they crawled back into the Jeep and headed for his old white house on Schavey Road thirty miles away. Kimberly remembered the last time she and Cort had driven through the dark toward that house. Then, it had only been five miles away, and then, she'd been nervous. Now, she was filled with a strange inner excitement, for tonight she knew exactly what she needed, what they both needed, to make their marriage a success.

Cort was vaguely aware of the country-western ballad playing softly over the radio. He supposed it added to the quiet intimacy inside the Jeep, but it wouldn't have mattered to him if the radio had been turned off. The sensuousness engulfing him couldn't have been stronger.

They'd stopped talking ten miles back. As the sun slowly inched its way lower in his rearview mirror, he became aware of the feminine scent clinging to Kimberly's clothes, and the woman-soft expression on her face every time she looked his way. She'd placed her hand on his knee five minutes ago. So far, he'd managed to keep the Jeep on the road.

A hundred thoughts scrambled through his mind, but only one sensation took hold deep in his body. He rotated his hips slightly, trying to loosen his jeans. But it was no use. A need had been building in him all day, growing each time she asked a question or offered him her opinion, each time she looked at him, temporal temptations written all over her face.

He'd congratulated himself on his restraint, telling himself he'd done a pretty bang-up job of holding his desire at bay. That restraint had never been tested more thoroughly than in that instant. The hand on his knee was warm, her touch soft and the tiniest bit trembly. But if he wasn't mistaken, it was gliding up his thigh, centimeter by slow centimeter. Any second now his self-control was going to go up in smoke, and so was he.

The closer he came to his place, the closer he came to placing his hand over hers and lifting it slightly higher. He grimaced to himself and shifted in the seat yet again.

"There's the house," she said, her voice little more than a husky whisper in the darkness.

Need pulsed through him anew. This time, there was no holding it back. Pulling into the driveway, he threw the lever into park and turned toward Kimberly.

"So," she asked, a note of shyness creeping into her voice, "would you say you like being married so far?"

"So far?" His voice cracked, but he couldn't help it.

"Yes. Um. I mean, you've only been a married man for one day, and I was just wondering how you thought things were going. So far."

Cort sucked in a quick breath and held it, wondering how in the hell her voice could have possibly sounded so breathless and shy while her fingers walked up his leg in an anything but shy manner.

"Cort?"

She'd whispered his name the exact moment her palm came into contact with the part of him begging for release. His arms went around her so fast neither of them had time to think. He lifted her, bodily, over the gearshift, settling the warm curve of her hip in the exact place her hand had been seconds earlier.

"Does this mean everything is okay so far?"

She'd done it again, going all warm and saucy and sexy as hell. "I'd say things are going a lot better than okay, Kimberly. Wouldn't you?" he asked huskily, the thrust of his hips emphasizing his statement like a roll of thunder.

"Oh, Cort."

It was all the answer he needed. He kissed her, long and hard and thoroughly. But it didn't take him long to realize that kissing just wasn't enough. Not by a long shot.

Need shot through him. Taking her hand, he helped her from the Jeep and led her toward the back step, his thoughts on one thing, and one thing only.

Chapter Seven

A tingle started at the back of Kimberly's neck, slowly shimmering lower until it reached her toes and started back up again. She'd shivered last night, too. But then, she'd blamed it on the rain. Tonight, the stars were out and there wasn't a cloud in sight. Tonight, she knew exactly what had caused those sensuous shivers. More specifically, she knew who.

That *who* kissed her the moment they stepped foot on the small back porch. As usual, Cort's kiss left her breathless and in need of so much more. They practically floated into the house where he wrapped his arms around her as if it had been months since he'd held her, instead of less than one day.

She'd caught him looking at her countless times today. He might have tried, but he couldn't seem to disguise his desire. She'd learned a great deal about the ranch, but she'd learned a lot more about Cort Sutherland. The man was stubborn, and had incredible self-control. He seemed to be one of those men she'd read about who found it difficult to voice his feelings outside of bed. Evidently, some women wanted to hear those precious words in another context. Kimberly didn't care *where* she heard them, as long as they were sincere.

Let it happen tonight, she whispered inside her head. *Let him tell me he loves me. Tonight.*

She was too new to the kitchen to make out any of the shadowy shapes in the darkness, but she recognized the sound of a door being kicked shut, and the sound of a huskily drawn breath of air. The next thing she knew, Cort was pulling her with him through the house. Although she couldn't see, she knew exactly where they were going. Even in their haste, she could hardly wait.

He kissed her at the foot of the bed, then made short work of removing her clothes. His breathing came in deep drafts, his movements more frenzied than ever before. His restraint seemed to be hanging by a thread. She knew, because this was the first time he'd ever forgotten to remove his hat.

She did it for him, whisking it from his head and tossing it away. It landed with a soft thud just as her eyes began to adjust to the darkness. He wrapped his arms around her and back-walked her around to the side of the bed where he lowered her to the mattress. He couldn't seem to do away with his own clothes fast enough. A button popped, a zipper rasped, a boot hit the floor with an impatient thud. And then he was as naked as she was, and his hands were gliding down her body, searching for pleasure points beyond her wildest imagination. She responded to him the way she always did, matching his movements, meeting the pace he set.

His hands kneaded and caressed, working magic, sending her thoughts careering and her desire soaring. He trailed kisses down her neck, cupping her breasts in his palms, his mouth following close behind.

He glided his hands down her body, and she moved, moaning his name. His hand stilled for but a moment. Yet something changed. It was almost imperceptible at first, but his restraint was back; his passion was controlled.

He was very considerate, tender, ardent. But when he drifted off to sleep this time, she was left with a niggling doubt that wouldn't be ignored.

He'd been careful. This was the second time. She wasn't sure why he felt it was necessary, but looking back, she knew the exact moment the change in him had occurred. He'd been incredible both nights, and both nights he'd slowed the pace seconds after placing his hands on her stomach, directly over the place where their baby was growing.

A warning voice whispered inside her head. Yes, he'd been careful. Not because he was in love with her, but because she was pregnant with his child.

She'd wondered what had happened to the wild passion he'd shown her that night months ago. Now she knew. The knowledge sent a sourness to the pit of her stomach that had nothing to do with morning sickness.

He married me because of the baby. And he was careful for the same reason.

A feeling of dread spread through her. If Cort didn't let himself go completely wild, abandoning all conscious thought, thereby getting lost in their lovemaking, how was he ever going to abandon himself to love?

What if he never did?

If that happened, Kimberly didn't know what she would do. But she didn't think she could live with a man who didn't love her. Not forever. Not even for her unborn child.

"Really, dear, these dishes won't know how to act if they're towel-dried. I've been letting them air-dry for years and years."

Kimberly picked up a faded yellow towel and reached for one of the plates her mother-in-law had just washed. "I don't mind. In fact, I'd rather have *something* to do."

"Feeling like a fish out of water, are you?"

Kimberly's mind jumped, and so did she, but other than the suspicious-looking smile pulling at her lips, Evelyn Sutherland appeared to be oblivious to Kimberly's gaping stare.

"Actually," Kimberly answered, measuring her words, "I have been feeling at loose ends during the day." Daytime wasn't the only time, but she thought it would be best to leave it at that.

"I don't know how you could feel any other way, what with all the changes that have taken place in your life recently," Evelyn declared, rinsing a handful of spoons and forks.

"Really?" Kimberly asked so fast she didn't have time to try to disguise the relief in her voice.

"My, yes. The first year of marriage is always difficult. There are just so many adjustments to make. Suddenly, there are two people sharing one house, one bathroom. And the decisions that must be dealt with—just how is a couple supposed to decide who sleeps on what side of the bed?"

Evelyn's wink made Kimberly smile, and relaxed her by degrees.

It had been this way all afternoon. She'd been a little nervous about coming over for dinner today. Although she'd caught Joe and Evelyn looking at her and Cort speculatively once or twice, the atmosphere in their country kitchen had been relaxed and friendly. Kimberly wasn't certain how coincidental it had been that Evelyn had served baked chicken instead of the beef Kimberly simply no longer had the heart to eat, but the smile on the older woman's face and the warmth in her eyes was as real as the primroses and violets blooming along the fences in the lane.

Cort and his father had gone outside to look at the new tractor. Kimberly had moved to follow and Evelyn had shrugged, saying, "If you want to see the new John Deere, go ahead. I've already seen it. Don't tell Joe I said this, but honestly, if you've seen one tractor, you've seen them all."

Smiling, and feeling like a conspirator, Kimberly had taken a quick peek at the tractor. It was big and shiny and complicated looking, but it didn't take her long to wander back into the house again. Now it was just the two of them inside, and Kimberly hadn't been sure what they'd talk about. She needn't have worried.

Evelyn Sutherland was slightly taller than Kimberly's five-foot-seven-inch frame. She was still slender, and at fifty-three, her dark hair was threaded with gray. Although she'd only known Cort's mother for a short time, Kimberly couldn't imagine her trying to cover her gray or worrying about wrinkles or makeup. The woman was beautiful the way she was, and appeared completely comfortable with herself. Kimberly admired that in a woman, and wished she had that kind of self-confidence.

Evelyn continued to list some of the adjustments newlyweds everywhere faced. Kimberly listened with one ear, but her mind wandered to a few of the adjustments she and Cort were trying to make. They'd been married for two weeks, their days falling into a comfortable pattern. He put in long hours on the ranch, coming into the house between six and seven, a bouquet of wildflowers in his hand more often than not. He took off his hat the same way every time—with his thumb and third finger—then hung it on a peg near the door. They prepared a meal together, or caught a movie and a bite to eat in town. They talked about the weather and the national news, discussed politics and religion, and made love nearly every night. But he hadn't lost himself completely, and he hadn't uttered one word about love.

"Why, the first year Joe and I were married we did more arguing than anything else. Well, almost anything else."

Evelyn's throaty laughter brought Kimberly back to the present.

"I can't say he was ever worried that I'd be unfaithful, but I once threatened to divorce him if he didn't start squeezing the toothpaste from the bottom of the tube."

Picking up a glass, Kimberly wondered if it was possible that part of what she and Cort were experiencing was normal. Maybe it was something all newlyweds went through.

"And do you know what?" Evelyn asked. "My threat didn't faze him. He knew I was crazy in love with him. What's worse, he taught Cort to do the same thing. Years later, I gave up trying to break that boy of the habit."

Kimberly stopped drying the glass in her hand and looked out the window where Joe and Cort appeared to be in the middle of an argument. They were squared off, shoulders rigid, hands on hips, heads shaking.

"Cort's as stubborn as a mule, all right."

Kimberly jerked her head around, suddenly realizing that she was talking to that mule's *mother*. Evelyn shook her head and made a huffing little sound, but she didn't look offended in the least.

"You've probably noticed that the boys come by their stubbornness naturally. The Sutherlands are a hardheaded lot, that's for sure. It takes a bighearted woman to love them, but they're worth it, Kimberly, so, so worth it."

Kimberly searched Evelyn's expression for hidden meaning, and found plenty. Letting her gaze trail back out the window where the argument appeared to be losing steam, she whispered, "I know, Evelyn. I know."

Evelyn heaved a huge sigh and said, "You don't know how relieved I am to hear you say that."

Hoping to gain a little insight, Kimberly asked, "What was Cort like as a child?"

Evelyn wiped her dripping hands on her apron, her expression changing in the subtlest of ways. "He was born during the last snowstorm in March and had dark wispy hair and a serious expression that he never truly lost. Will was only fourteen months older, and was a corker from day one. Not Cort. His eyes were always watchful, his actions calculated. And questions. Good Lord, that boy was full of questions. He wanted to know how everything worked, how to take it apart and put it together again."

Kimberly was so lost in the images Evelyn's words evoked she didn't know how they ended up sitting around the old oak table, sipping lemonade. She watched Evelyn smooth her hand over the table's work-worn surface, amazed at the tenderness in her expression, and in the gentleness in those chapped hands.

"Cort probably hasn't had a chance to tell you this yet, but I always wanted a houseful of children. Boys or girls, handsome, pretty or plain. It never mattered. Unfortunately, my body wasn't built for childbearing. Will and Cort were both large babies, their deliveries difficult. The doctor told us to wait a while before trying for a third. So, Joe and I waited. Three years later, I had a miscarriage very early in the pregnancy. A year later, it happened again. Two years went by, and I was aching to hold another baby in my arms. This time, I was extra careful, but it was still a difficult pregnancy from the very beginning. More difficult than any of the others."

One of Kimberly's hands flew to her mouth, the other to her stomach. "What happened?"

Evelyn's eyes grew large and wary. "Oh, dear, I didn't mean to tell you this. Don't you worry, your baby is going to be just fine. You're literally glowing with good health. I've seen how strong you are, and how much energy you have. I was so sickly and weak during the entire pregnancy I couldn't even open the lid on my canned peaches. I went into labor when I was barely seven months along. Anne Elizabeth Sutherland was born on a beautiful fall day. She lived for twelve hours, and spent most of her life in our arms."

A tear rolled down Kimberly's face. "Cort would have been seven."

Evelyn smiled sadly. "He told me you were good with numbers."

"Oh, Evelyn, I'm so sorry."

"So am I, dear, even after all this time. If you don't mind my saying so myself, I would have been a wonderful mother to that little girl."

Smiling through her tears, Kimberly caught a glimpse of Cort in his mother's expression. "I think so, too. What did you do, after those twelve hours, I mean?"

"We went on. I know it sounds trite, but we got through it a day at a time. The pregnancy was hard on me physically and emotionally, and the doctors told us there weren't going to be any more babies. Sometimes, I think it was even harder on Joe. He blamed himself. Said he should have been inside more, helping with the boys and the cleaning and the cooking. Of course, there was nothing he could have done. But do you know what, Kimberly?"

Kimberly sniffled and shook her head.

"Good things come to those who wait. After all these years, I'm getting the large family I've always wanted. Not only do we have two good, healthy, wonderful sons, but we have two beautiful daughters-in-law, an adorable grandson and another grandchild on the way."

Kimberly swiped at her damp cheeks and nodded, so many things becoming clear. She could almost picture Cort as he would have been that long-ago summer, his eyes huge, his expression serious as he tiptoed through a silent house that should have been filled with oohs and aahs and a baby's tiny cry.

No wonder Cort was so careful with her. He didn't want a repeat performance. But this wasn't the same at all. She wasn't having a difficult pregnancy. She was as healthy as a horse, and one of these days she'd be as big as one, too. But she wasn't very big, not yet. And she wanted her husband. Now that she understood him a little better, she was going to have him. She just wasn't sure how.

But she'd figure it out. She was a genius, after all.

Kimberly stepped onto the tiny back porch, her hands automatically settling to her upper arms where the evening chill brought goose bumps to her skin. In the distance Cort was silhouetted against the last remaining swirls of color in the sky. He was sitting on the fence as if he'd been born to it. His back was to her, his arms raised, a rope twirling in a circle over his head. The lasso hovered in the sky as if suspended in time, then whipped out and closed around a post several yards away.

He slid off the fence in one fluid motion. Ambling to the post, he slipped the lasso off and wound the rope neatly in his left hand. By the time he'd returned to his perch, Kimberly was leaning on the wooden fence a few feet away.

"Evenin'," he called.

She folded her arms over the top board and said, "You're very polite, aren't you?"

"My mother's doing, not mine."

She smiled at his irreverent expression. "Are you having fun?"

He gave her a loose-jointed shrug and said, "The problem with fence posts is they don't come when you rope 'em."

She shook her head, watching as he secured his foothold on a lower board, then once again took the rope in his right hand.

"What did you and my mother talk about this afternoon?" he asked, twirling the rope over his head.

"Oh, lots of things. She told me about her courtship with your father, and how you once disassembled the carburetor on his tractor when you were five years old."

"You must have been bored to death."

"Actually, I enjoyed every minute. Now it's your turn. What did you and your father argue about?"

He jerked his head around so fast she thought he might fall off the fence. But the rope stayed in the air, and after he righted himself he said, "What?"

"When the two of you were nose to nose in the driveway after supper."

"Oh, that. We weren't arguing. That's the way we discuss things."

Kimberly shook her head at his lofty tone. The rope sailed out again and, with a flick of Cort's wrist, closed around its mark.

"You're very good at that," she said quietly.

"Timing is everything."

He slipped off the fence again. Kimberly stayed where she was, his simple statement echoing through her mind. *Timing is everything.* How simple yet eloquent. He might not have realized it, but she agreed with him. Timing *was* everything, in roping, and in relationships, too.

She'd done a lot of thinking about this since her conversation with Cort's mother. As usual, she'd thought until her head ached, but she'd come to a few conclusions. She and

Cort had begun their relationship in the middle, instead of at the beginning. They'd gone to bed together when they should have been having their first date, and got married when they should have been having their third. No wonder everything seemed out of kilter for them now.

It seemed that it was up to her to right the situation. The question was how?

She wasn't sure about everything yet, but she knew she had to slow things down between them, go back to the basics, back to the beginning, back to what drew them to each other in the first place, before there was a baby to worry about, and to love. They had to get to know each other in the true sense of the word. If they were ever going to create a loving home for their child, that's what they had to do.

When Cort's rope closed around its target the third time in a row, she asked, "Who taught you to do that?"

"An old man who came looking for work a long time ago. I was eight years old and was convinced he was at least a hundred. He could swear out of one side of his mouth and spit out of the other. But he said he was the best roper within a five-state radius. And I believed him."

"What was his name?"

"He never said. But everyone calls him Pokey."

A warm glow went through Kimberly, chasing away the chill in the evening air. This was what she'd meant about starting over at the beginning. This warm camaraderie and quiet sharing was what they needed if they were going to forge a lasting bond and an unwavering commitment.

She climbed up onto the fence, her knees facing out, Cort's facing in, less than an arm's length between their bent elbows. Feeling slightly dizzy, she focused on the lit kitchen window, waiting for the sensation to pass.

It was so different out here. There were no sirens wailing, no traffic, no honking horns or raised voices. There was just her and Cort on a fence on a quiet May night. It was too early for insects, and too late in the season for howling winds. To Kimberly, it seemed like a magical time when anything was possible. Even winning her husband's love.

She'd sat in nearly the same place yesterday, watching the cowhands clip their horses' hooves and reshoe them. Mo and Frank hadn't said much, but Pokey had grinned and nodded and patiently explained what he was doing. The look in his eyes said he'd seen a lot in all his decades of living.

"Did Pokey tell you I talked to him yesterday?" she asked.

"Nope. But that isn't surprising. He can go days without saying more than three words, then spend the next eight hours talking nonstop."

"He's quite a character, isn't he? But if he seemed a hundred all those years ago, how old he is now?"

"I've never been able to pin him down, but he claims he's sixty-something. Of course, he's been claiming the same thing for at least a dozen years."

If voices could smile, Cort's would be doing just that. An answering grin settled on her mouth and, if she wasn't mistaken, around her heart.

"So he just showed up one day and stayed?" she asked quietly.

Cort let the rope hang slack, one end in his hand, the other fastened around a post on the other side of the corral. His voice, when it came, was filled with a strange mixture of reverence and exasperation she'd never heard him use before.

"It was my father who actually hired him, my father who saw beyond the bandy legs and chew, which just goes to prove that my dad has *always* been able to see what was on the inside of a person. Anyway, Pokey said he was born in Texas, but his cowboying took him to Colorado and Wyoming, and eventually brought him here. Nobody's ever given me a harder time about anything, not even my father and Will. And nobody's ever taught me more about ranching, about herding cattle and about camp fires under the stars."

It seemed to her that Cort Sutherland had had a charmed life, in spite of the loss of his baby sister. She wanted to broach that particular subject, but before she could find the proper words, he asked, "Did I ever tell you about the trophy I once won for roping calves at the state fair?"

She cast him an arched look he probably couldn't see in the gathering darkness. "Let me get this straight. Your father taught you to *discuss,* Pokey taught you to rope and your mother taught you to say please. Who, exactly, taught you to brag?"

He pulled the rope tight and strummed it like a huge guitar string. Leaning closer, he whispered, "Like I said, it ain't bragging if you can really do it."

Kimberly went warm inside, her joints heating up and her thoughts turning to liquid. At times like this when the day was almost over and it seemed as if they were the only two people on earth, she could almost believe that Cort was coming to love her.

She felt his advance as much as saw it. His face came closer, the heat of his body wrapping around her like a dream. And then his lips touched hers. Her eyes fluttered closed, and she had to hold on to the fence with both hands to keep from sliding off and landing in a heap on the ground below.

He changed the angle of the kiss, parting his lips slightly and moving them across hers. With her head still spinning, she pulled back the tiniest bit, keeping the joining of their mouths as weightless as a sigh.

He raised his face from hers. And neither of them spoke. They just looked at each other, their eyes opened wide, their hearts thumping in a rhythm all their own.

Leaning closer, he whispered, "Why don't we go inside where it's warmer, and where I can kiss you more thoroughly."

Her heart practically turned over. Unfortunately, her head spun and her temples throbbed. Placing a hand to her forehead, she whispered, "It sounds wonderful, Cort, but I think I'd better just go on in alone. I know it sounds trite, but I'm tired tonight. I think I'll turn in early. If you don't mind."

Cort, who'd been balancing on fences since he was old enough to walk, almost fell off for the second time that night. He managed to right himself without losing too much dignity, then said, "Are you sure you're feeling all right?"

"I have a little headache, but mostly I'm just tired, like I said."

"Oh. Well. I'll help you inside."

"No, really," she said. "I'm fine. There's nothing to do except wash my face and brush my teeth and crawl into bed. And I'm sure I can handle those on my own. But, Cort?"

"Hmm?"

"I just wanted to say thanks. For today. It's been wonderful. I'll see you in the morning."

He turned around and watched Kimberly sashay into the house. Her pale yellow slacks and oversize shirt appeared white against the blackness of night. Even though she was three and a half months along, her body was still thin, her legs long and lean. Her breasts were slightly larger, and her stomach wasn't completely flat anymore. As far as he was concerned, it only added to her beauty. The thought of her lush curves sent an ache all the way through him.

The light came on in their bedroom. Five minutes later, it went out again.

He swung off the fence and ambled over to the post to free his lasso. Winding the rope up in his hand, he again looked at the windows of the house. This was the first time Kimberly had refused his advances. He knew better than to take her rejection personally. If she said she was tired, he believed her. But he still felt lonely standing out there in the dark with nothing but his rope for company.

He practiced his lassoing skills several more times, but his concentration had been broken, and he missed his target more often than not. It wasn't surprising, considering how many times his eyes strayed to that darkened window.

Kimberly was probably already asleep, curled up on her side, her hair smoothed over her pillow. He wondered what she'd do if he tiptoed into the room and woke her. He wouldn't make any noise, and he certainly wouldn't shake her. He would just stand and watch her sleep for a little while. Maybe he'd lean down and glide a finger along her cheek, and run it down her arm. If he brushed the outside of her breasts, it would be purely accidental. And if she awakened and turned into his touch...

Desire pounded through him, settling below his belt. He stared at the house, imagining her on the other side of that wall, right there in his bed, ripe for the taking. But she was tired, and needed her sleep.

He turned in a circle and looked around, wondering if he should take a long, hard walk, or a cold, vigorous shower. In the end, he did both. Unfortunately, neither of them had the lasting effect he'd hoped for.

"Cort, I'm fine. Really. I'm sure it's nothing serious. It's probably just a case of the twenty-four-hour flu. You can go mend your fences or rope your cattle or do whatever it is you're supposed to do today."

He pressed his work-roughened hand to her face. "You still have a fever."

She settled back into the pillows, feeling incredibly tired but trying not to let it show. "It's under a hundred. And I haven't been sick in more than two hours. The worst is over."

"I don't like this. I don't like it at all."

Kimberly knew she must look a sight, but smiled at him, anyway. After all, Cort, the poor baby, looked worse than she did. His eyes were red rimmed where he'd rubbed them all night, and the lower half of his face was covered with the dark stubble of a day-old beard.

Now that she knew about the disastrous outcome of his mother's last pregnancy, she found his overprotectiveness endearing. He'd been wonderful throughout the entire night, holding her hair away from her face while she bent over the commode, tucking the blankets around her neck each time she crawled back into bed, placing a cool cloth to her forehead. She'd been on her own for a long time, and his quiet vigilance had been comforting. But she was better now, and enough was enough.

"Well," she said, muffling a yawn, "you're welcome to hover over me if you want to, but I'm going to take a little nap. I'll probably be as good as new when I wake up. Good night. Or should I say good morning?"

Cort didn't know how anyone could drift off to sleep so effortlessly. Kimberly did it before his very eyes. He stood watching her sleep for a time. He paced to the door and back again, cursing the floor for creaking. He felt agitated. And it had nothing to do with loose floorboards.

Kimberly had been violently ill last night, even though she'd claimed it wasn't anything serious. He'd been there, dammit, and saw how her body had racked and contorted each time she retched.

She did look better this morning. She was keeping juice and ice chips down now. Her color was back, and her face felt cooler. He still would have preferred to bundle her into his truck and drive her to the emergency room in the hospital in North Platte.

It had been little more than two weeks since he'd taken his wedding vows, and he hadn't planned to have them put to the test so soon. But he'd learned a thing or two about "in sickness and in health" during those long hours in the night. He'd learned a thing or two about Kimberly, too. She was a lot more stubborn than she let on. He'd wanted to call her doctor. She'd insisted she just had a touch of the flu. She'd even pointed to a chapter in one of her prenatal books to reassure him that her symptoms weren't life threatening or even all that serious. As the hours passed, her symptoms *did* lessen, and she was able to sleep. Still, he'd kept vigil in the chair by the bed, and sometime between four and five in the morning, he made her a promise she didn't hear.

He'd never been a man who took his responsibilities lightly, and he wasn't about to start now. He was going to take care of this woman. His wife.

He was going to make her happy.

And he was going to keep her and the baby safe. If it was the last thing he ever did.

The barn smelled of fresh straw. It wasn't exactly the stuff romantic movies were made of, but looking at the glittering bits of dust riding on a slanted beam of sunlight, and hearing the birds singing in the trees outside, Kimberly decided that candlelight and violins were overrated. Spring was in the air, and so was romance. She could feel it.

Cort had driven into the driveway a few minutes ago, gravel churning beneath his truck's wheels as he'd climbed on the brakes. He'd disappeared inside the house before she could poke her head out of the barn door.

"I'm here, Cort!" she called the moment he set foot on the back step. "In the barn."

She couldn't make out his expression from here, especially not the part of his face shaded by his hat. But there was no grimness in the set of his shoulders, and his gait was that of a man who was happy to see her.

He ambled toward her just as he had countless times these past two days since she'd been sick. He always claimed he had a good reason for his surprise visits. He needed something or other from one of the outbuildings, or he had to make a phone call. But she knew he was really checking on her. How could she complain? She loved seeing him in the middle of the day, and the fact that she was on his mind so often filled her with a budding happiness. There was one little problem.

He *had* finally gone outside that morning when she'd had the flu, but he'd come back into the bedroom every fifteen minutes. Evelyn came over with a pot of homemade soup at lunchtime. And Krista showed up around three. It was a wonder she'd managed to get any rest at all, but by evening she was feeling so much better she took a long bubble bath and washed her hair. Feeling warm, cherished almost, she'd curled up close to her husband, ready to take up where they'd left off the previous night. He'd covered her wandering fingertips with his hand, his message gentle but firm. They shouldn't make love so soon after she'd been sick.

They hadn't made love since.

She'd wanted to go back to the basics where their relationship was concerned. But she hadn't meant *that* far back. She wanted to have a normal marriage, one based on mutual respect and friendship. And passion.

"Are you getting to know the horses?"

Cort's voice drew her from her reveries. He'd stopped in the barn's doorway, his tall, lanky body a dark outline against the bright sun.

"I've been talking to Misty."

He took a few steps closer and tipped up the brim of his hat. "Have you been telling her your life story?"

"Why, does she look sleepy?"

He obviously knew better than answer that question one way or the other.

"Cort, I want to learn to ride her."

"I don't think that would be a good idea, not when you've never ridden before. Especially now, Kim."

He'd called her Kim, and even though she didn't like the rest of what he'd said, it was happening again. He could turn her inside out with a look, but when he called her Kim, her knees grew weak and her mind turned to thistledown.

Sauntering closer, she said, "I'd be careful, and I wouldn't try anything fancy. Just a nice stroll around the corral."

"It's too dangerous."

Egad, the man was stubborn. Trying another tact, she went back to the stall and stroked the old mare's head. "She's as docile as a lamb. How old is she?"

"Fifteen."

Wavering him a slow, secret smile, she said, "They say dogs age seven years to every one of ours. If horses do the same, she'd be a hundred and five years old. I hardly think she'd be dangerous, do you? Besides, I have to find something to do with my time."

"Then you're feeling better?"

She took one step toward him, and then another. "Don't I look better?"

Cort swallowed. Hard. He didn't know what Kimberly was up to, but something told him that she knew exactly how she looked. Beautiful and serene and sexy as hell.

"Well?" she asked.

"You definitely look better. In fact, I'd say you look very healthy and maternal."

She paused, a strange expression on her face. Striding past her, he was aware of her eyes on him, but he remained steadfast in the promise he'd made to her the night she'd been sick.

He lifted the saddle from the rack and heaved it into position on Rambler's back. With quick, sure movements, he tightened the cinch and put on the bridle, then grabbed the reins and led his horse outside.

"Where are you going?" she asked.

He swung up into the saddle, slipped his feet into the stirrups and adjusted his hat. "Today's been one of those days when whatever could go wrong did go wrong. The new bull broke out. It took four men on horseback to get the ornery cuss corralled again. And Dad flagged me down on the road west of his place. One of the tractors I rebuilt last winter broke down in the middle of the north eighty acres."

"Then you're going to help him fix it?" she asked.

"I already did."

"Then where are you going?"

"Some fences need mending."

"Now?"

The breeze chose that instant to flutter through her clothing and trail several strands of her golden blond hair across her face. She smoothed them back, her wedding ring glinting in the sun. If Cort had believed in signs from above, he'd say he'd just had one.

"You said you're feeling okay."

"I am."

"Then I'd better get to work. I'll be home at the usual time. I'll take you out to supper. There's a diner over in

Calloway we haven't tried yet. If you'd rather eat someplace else, just let me know when I get home.''

Without another word, he rode off at a gallop into the sunset. At least it would have been into the sunset if it hadn't been four in the afternoon.

As Rambler's hooves churned up the dust in the lane, Cort told himself his quick departure had nothing to do with the woman-soft smile on Kimberly's lips. And it certainly didn't have anything to do with how she looked in her blue jumpsuit. She'd said it was one of her new maternity outfits. If that was true, it must have been made out of fabric that would stretch, because it fit her lithe body like a glove.

No, neither of those things had anything to do with the reason he'd saddled up Rambler and headed down the lane. Just because it was getting more and more difficult to resist Kimberly didn't mean he was running away.

There really were fences to mend. Somewhere.

Chapter Eight

Kimberly raised her hand to knock, then hesitated, torn by conflicting emotions. She'd thought long and hard about coming to Krista's today, and had practiced her oration a hundred times.

She was going to be straightforward and up-front and professional. She would hold her head high and calmly say, *"Krista, I seem to be having a little problem and since you've always been more earthy and sensuous than me, I was wondering if you'd mind giving me a tip or two on ways to seduce my husband."*

Running a hand over her forehead, she took a deep breath for courage and rapped soundly on the door. Krista opened it within seconds, and all Kimberly's carefully rehearsed words stuck in her throat. All she could manage was a tense little smile.

"Kimberly," Krista exclaimed. "Come on in! Last night I told Katrina that I'd give you one more day, and if I still hadn't heard from you, I was going to drive over to your place so I could see for myself that you're okay."

Please, not someone else checking up on her health.

Following Krista into her sunny kitchen, she asked, "Katrina's been calling you?"

"Three times this week alone."

That sounded like Katrina. "I'm surprised she didn't call me herself. What did you tell her?"

Krista's dark eyes lit up as she said, "I told her you'd had a little touch of the flu, but were feeling as good as new. I also explained that you were married to a Sutherland. Therefore, it wasn't unusual that you hadn't surfaced yet."

Kimberly felt her cheeks color, and knew that this was the perfect time to pour out her secret. If only she could have remembered where she'd left her courage.

"Kimberly, you are feeling all right, aren't you?"

"Yes, of course. The flu only lasted twelve hours. I'm fine."

Krista's eyes narrowed, uncertainty creeping into her expression. "Then how about something to drink? Can you stomach coffee yet?"

"I can't even say it out loud."

She grimaced to herself. *Obviously, coffee wasn't the only thing.*

"I couldn't drink coffee the entire time I was expecting Tommy. But don't worry. It passed."

"Really?"

Krista nodded, and suddenly Kimberly was glad she'd come, even if she couldn't bring herself to say what was on her mind.

"Go on into the living room," Krista said. "I'll bring us something to drink that tastes nothing like c-o-f-f-e-e."

Kimberly stopped inside the arched doorway and slowly looked around. This was the room where she'd first seen Cort again on Tommy's seventh birthday more than a month ago. It was also the room in which she'd become Cort's wife. Today, there were no birthday ribbons and wrapping paper flying through the air, and no wedding candles flickering on the mantel.

She strode into the room, running her hand along the back of the overstuffed sofa, peering at framed photographs and knickknacks. Tommy's baseball glove and several balls filled a woven basket, the tip of one of his shoes peeking from the ruffle of a comfortable-looking chair.

Glasses clinked on a tray behind her, signaling Krista's arrival into the room. Glancing over her shoulder, Kimberly asked, "Were you born knowing how to make a house a home?"

Krista placed the tray on a wicker coffee table before answering. "I've always been determined to give Tommy the security of a loving, comfortable home. And I like to think I succeeded, for the most part. But this is different," she said, spreading her hands wide enough to encompass the entire room. "Will and I are turning this house into a home together, just as you and Cort will do with the old house on Schavey Road."

Kimberly didn't have the heart or the courage to tell Krista that she wasn't sure the house on Schavey Road would ever be her home.

"So tell me," Krista said, smiling and radiant. "What have you been doing this week? During the day, I mean."

The glint in those dark eyes said she already had a good idea what Kimberly had been doing at night. Kimberly crossed her arms, pretending to study a group of framed photographs on a shelf. She'd spent a good portion of her days cleaning and organizing. Hideous, tedious tasks. But at least it had given her something to do with her time. As a result, the house was spotless, the drawers in Cort's desk neat, his ledgers balanced, his filing up-to-date.

Cort came inside every night between six and seven. They prepared dinner together, or went out for supper and a movie. They ended each day with a kiss, and nothing more, and each night, she became more and more worried that he'd never completely abandon himself to the whirl of passion, or to love.

Her desperation was growing into a kind of weighted sorrow that sat like a knot in her stomach, rising to her throat without warning. It was why she'd come here today. It was too bad she couldn't bring herself to voice her fears.

Maybe if she and Krista had been close all their lives, she could have asked for her advice. Or maybe some things weren't meant to be discussed.

"Kimberly?"

"Hmm?"

"You're miles away."

Kimberly swallowed, suddenly remembering Krista's last question. "You wanted to know what I've been doing? My things arrived from Boston yesterday."

"Then you've probably been unpacking."

"I've done some, but I have to do it during the day when Cort isn't around. He doesn't want me lifting anything heavier than my hand." Her smile felt out of place on her own mouth.

"I've noticed he's very protective."

Kimberly nodded without turning around. "I loved the furnishings in my town house in Boston. Now I don't know. My lamps and vases and bookends don't seem to mesh with Cort's things."

"Maybe some things just take time."

Kimberly glanced around, straight into Krista's eyes. Her sister, younger by little more than a year, was very intuitive. Kimberly suddenly felt like crying. Turning her attention back to a photograph she hadn't seen in years, she asked, "Krista, do you ever miss our father?"

Krista moved closer, her shoulder brushing Kimberly's. "For a long time I felt cheated."

"I think we all did," Kimberly said quietly. "But at least you were home with Mother and had a more normal childhood. Katrina, Kendra and I barely knew her until we were adults."

Krista nodded. "That's why it's always been so important to me to give Tommy a childhood that's as normal as possible."

Bit by bit, Kimberly was beginning to realize that she and Krista had more in common than she used to think. They both missed the father they hardly remembered. They both knew their mother had done her best, and they both wanted their children to grow up strong and healthy and happy. Their father's early death had been out of anyone's control. But *her* child had a father.

Maybe happiness wasn't completely out of her reach, after all. Maybe she was just going to have to try harder with Cort. But how? What could she do?

"She has the look of a woman who's been thoroughly kissed, don't you think?"

Kimberly's eyebrows went up, her gaze darting from Krista's face to the framed snapshot of their parents. "Who, Mother?"

"Yes, Mother. She was more than our mother to him, you know. And look at the expression on Dad's face."

Kimberly studied the photo of her parents. The picture had been taken nearly thirty years ago. Even though it wasn't in color, the emotions in her parents' eyes were vivid. "Katrina, Kendra and I look a lot like her, don't we?"

"And I look like him."

"I think you inherited Dad's earthy sensuality, too," Kimberly said quietly.

"I'm not the only one who snagged that particular gene, Kimberly."

"What makes you say that?"

"How could I be the only one when both of our parents carried it? You and I weren't the only women in our family to be carried away by passion, you know."

"You mean our prim and proper mother—"

"Seduced our father," Krista cut in.

"But Mother always seemed so polished, polite and reserved."

"She was all those things," Krista said. "But there was more to her personality than that. A few months before she died, I glimpsed bits and pieces of an entirely different woman. Even though she was extremely tired and weak near the end, her eyes lit up each time she mentioned our father. They were completely in love with each other and had a whirlwind courtship. You didn't think having four children in five years was all his idea, did you?"

Kimberly stared at the photograph. Her memories of her father were vague, but she conjured up the image of a man with a deep voice and strong arms, a man who liked spicy foods, and loved to laugh. But Krista was saying that their mother was sensuous, too—their mother, whose skin was pale, her eyes blue and serene. Looking closer at the woman in the picture, Kimberly saw that there was more than serenity in her mother's eyes, and her lips *did* glisten with wetness and *did* look surprisingly full.

"But why did Mother feel it was necessary to seduce our father?" Kimberly asked.

"Because she was from a proper Eastern family, and his family owned a spaghetti restaurant in Michigan. He thought she deserved better. She had other ideas."

Staring at the mother she'd hardly known, Kimberly wondered if it was possible that Krista was on to something here. Maybe blue-eyed blondes could be every bit as earthy and sensuous as brown-eyed brunettes.

Newfound confidence radiated from her heart to the tips of her fingers. If their mother had deemed it necessary to take matters into her own hands and seduce the man she loved, maybe Kimberly should do the same thing.

"If I'm reading the expression on your face accurately," Krista said with a gentle nudge, "I'd say that brother-in-law of mine doesn't stand a chance."

"You know something, Krista?" Kimberly asked, her mind already methodically calling up and discarding ideas. "I think you might be right."

They looked at each other. And started to laugh.

"That's as strong a heartbeat as I've ever heard," Dr. Bradley Grady, OB-GYN, declared.

"Oh, Cort, listen."

Kimberly heard the wonder in her own voice and knew her eyes must have been huge. She was lying on a table, her slacks pushed down to her hips, a stethoscope that was hooked to a special amplifier pressed to her belly. Cort stood on one side of the examining table, his hat in one hand, the fingers of his other hand entwined with hers. And all around them, the baby's heart beat a magnificent rhythm.

"It sounds like the hooves of a half-grown colt galloping down the lane."

Cort's voice was husky, and was filled with so much of his own brand of awe it sent tears to Kimberly's eyes. As far as she was concerned, the sound of their baby's heartbeat was the most beautiful sound in the world, and the look on Cort's face was the most magnificent.

As always, his face was shaped by strong angles and dark hollows. The cleft in his chin was more pronounced beneath the bright overhead lighting, the glint in his eyes more apparent. The enormity of her feelings for him filled her with so much inner excitement she felt giddy. And Kimberly Wilson Sutherland could count on one hand the times in her life when she'd felt giddy.

She'd caught Cort looking at her strangely several times these past few days. He didn't seem to know what to make of her infinite good cheer and soft, knowing smiles. She planned to let him in on her secret. Very soon.

She'd been extremely busy since her visit with Krista, but she'd always been the happiest when her mind was active. It was no wonder Cort watched her when he thought she wasn't looking. He probably didn't know what to make of the new glint in her eyes or the perpetual hum on her lips.

But he would.

She'd driven straight into North Platte after leaving Krista's house last week, and made a beeline for the library. Now that she thought about it, she wondered why it hadn't occurred to her sooner. She'd always loved books, so it seemed only natural that she'd turn to them for advice now.

The North Platte Library wasn't huge, but it had a surprisingly thorough section that dealt with human sensuality. As a result, tucked under her bed this very minute were books dealing with everything from seduction to erogenous zones to one hundred and one positions.

Willing the twitch of her lips not to give her thoughts away, she said, "Then everything is all right with the baby, Dr. Grady?"

The instant the doctor lifted the stethoscope from her abdomen, the room became a quiet background for Dr. Grady's deep voice. "This baby is perfectly healthy, Mrs. Sutherland, and so are you."

Kimberly's smile broadened. She tugged at her clothing and, with her hand already in Cort's, casually pulled herself to a sitting position. Everything was going according to plan. She'd been to the doctor two weeks ago, and was only scheduled to see him once a month for the time being. But she'd made a special appointment today so that Cort could meet him, and see for himself that she and the baby were both strong and healthy and in absolutely no physical danger.

Casting a covert glance at the doctor, she said, "What about, um, intimacy?"

"What about it?" Dr. Grady asked with mock seriousness.

She let go of Cort's hand on the pretense of smoothing a wrinkle from her slacks. What she really needed was some other place to look, and something to do with her hands.

"What I mean is, um— Or rather, what I'm trying to say is..."

"Are you trying to ask about having sex?"

She nodded, but she didn't allow anything to divert her gaze from the good doctor's. Not even Cort's gasp.

"By all means," Dr. Grady said. "A good, healthy sex life won't harm you or the baby in the least."

She'd liked the middle-aged doctor the moment she saw him. Now, she could have kissed him.

"Thank you, Doctor," she said. "You've been most helpful. Now, Cort? Are you ready to go?"

His gaze roamed her entire face, settling on her mouth. She felt herself blushing, but she was too busy smiling and making plans to care.

* * *

Kimberly was still smiling two hours later. She couldn't help it. She'd noticed Cort looking at her during lunch. There was a time when she might have averted her gaze, but that was the old Kimberly. The new Kimberly proudly held his open stare.

There was a sensuous glimmer in his eyes she hadn't seen in quite a while. An answering awareness started at the back of her neck and slowly shimmered lower. The visit to Dr. Grady had changed something in their relationship. She felt closer to her husband than ever before. They'd shared the first sound of their baby's heartbeat, and in the process, they were forging a bond that very well could be the basis for their entire relationship.

"Look at that sky."

She glanced first at Cort, then at the sky he'd mentioned. She'd taken a meteorology class once, so she could name every kind of cloud on the horizon. But what pleased her even more was the fact that she was coming to recognize the subtle nuances in her husband's personality. She could tell by the set of his chin and the squareness of his shoulders what kind of a day he'd had. Cort Sutherland was a stubborn man who enjoyed a good argument and could go head-to-head with the orneriest of God's creatures when it suited him. But his anger was always restrained to slamming a door or shouldering his way into a wooden gate.

His restraint wasn't confined to the outdoors. She practically snorted at the vastness of that understatement. Oh, no, he'd shown her just how much control he had over himself each time they'd made love since their wedding day.

But it wasn't going to last. She could feel it. A storm might have been brewing somewhere out over the Sand Hills, but it was nothing compared to the one she had in store for her husband.

He turned onto the road leading to Krista's house, the momentum of the car bringing her into close contact with his body. She stayed where she was, even after he'd completed the turn, silently wishing she hadn't promised Krista that she'd be there when Tommy got off the bus this afternoon. Kimberly would have much rather gone straight home.

"Did Krista say what time she'll be back?" Cort asked in a tone of voice that mirrored her own longings.

Sighing, Kimberly said, "She wasn't scheduled to work this afternoon, but one of the other physical therapists got sick and asked her to fill in. But she said she'd be back by suppertime. I'll have her bring me straight home."

She couldn't quite bring herself to press her hand to his cheek, but she leaned ahead slightly, offering her mouth for his kiss. She thought it was mighty nice of him to comply so readily. But then, Cort Sutherland was a nice man. He was also virile, his kisses filled with so much impatience and open longing she could hardly think.

Their lips parted, and her eyes opened. Sighing again, she said, "I guess I'll see you later."

She got out on her own side before he could help her. Standing back, she waved. He waved back hesitantly, as if he didn't quite know what to make of the new *her*.

Yes, she thought to herself. It would have been nice if they could have gone right home. Straight home and straight to bed.

Later, she said to herself. *There would be plenty of time later. In fact, later, they'd have all night.*

With anticipation swelling her chest, and a feeling of rightness settling everywhere else, she strode into her sister's house to wait for Tommy to get home from school.

She hung up the phone an hour later, feeling infinitely sure of herself and her rightful place in the universe. Even the call she'd taken from Katrina couldn't dampen her anticipation. Her older sister was a master at asking pointed questions. Kimberly had been careful not to give out any more information than she felt comfortable with, but some of those questions had made her even more sure of her strategy.

Cort was on the verge of discovering that he was in love with her. She had nothing but women's intuition to bank her feelings on, but, as she was slowly learning, women's intuition could go where numeric equations had never gone.

She intended to continue in her unwavering quest for her husband's love. She *had* gotten her courage up enough to put her hand on his knee that day weeks ago. But that had been spontaneous. This was premeditated seduction.

Heading out the back door to check on Tommy, she listed all the givens in her relationship with Cort. He cared about her. He wanted her. And if he'd let himself, he could love her the way she loved him. She was just going to have to continue to find ways to rope him in.

Shading her eyes with her hand, she spotted Tommy. He was sitting on an overturned bucket, a miniature cowboy hat on his head, a rope in his hand, and Blue, his overgrown puppy, sitting at his side. She reached him at the same time his lasso closed around one of his stuffed bears, which just happened to be the same instant an idea took shape in her mind.

"You're pretty good at that."

"Not as good as Uncle Cort," he said, reeling the teddy bear in.

"Is that who taught you to lasso?"

"Yep."

Going down on her knees near her only nephew, she asked, "Do you think you could teach me?"

"Why not?" he asked. "We're both geniuses, aren't we?"

She ruffled his hair, shaking her head at his loftiness.

An hour later she clapped the dust from her hands and handed the rope back to Tommy. "Thanks, kiddo. I think that'll do it."

He eyed her curiously. "I never woulda thought one of the aunts would want to learn about roping."

She laughed out loud, and couldn't resist giving him a hug. "We never know when a skill might come in handy, now, do we?"

Tommy squinted up at her as if he wasn't quite sure what to make of the uncharacteristic glint in her eyes. They both turned at the sound of a car pulling into the driveway. Krista was back, which meant that Kimberly could go home and set her plan into motion.

Strengthened by her newly awakened courage and determination, she called goodbye to Tommy and set off to do what she had to do.

Cort pulled the Jeep to a stop near his back door and got out. He'd told Mo, Frank and Pokey he'd help them get ready to do the branding. He hadn't planned to stop by the house, had, in fact, only driven out here to Schavey Road because they needed the irons from the barn. But now that he was here, he couldn't seem to fight the overwhelming desire to pop in and say hello to Kim before heading back out again.

She looked up from the stove before he made it all the way inside. She was cooking something in a rounded pan that must have arrived with her things from Boston.

"Hello," she called with a woman-soft voice that almost buckled his knees.

"Something smells good."

"I'm just sautéing the shrimp, but I was planning to start the stir-fry in half an hour. Unless you're hungry now."

Stir-fry. So that's what she was cooking.

"That's okay," he said, sauntering closer. "I just happened to be in the neighborhood, so I stopped in to say hello."

"Your timing's perfect, but then, it seems to me that someone once told me that timing's everything."

Cort swallowed, letting his hands settle on his hips. There was something different about Kim these days. He'd always glimpsed tenderness in her expression, but lately he'd noticed an underlying sensuality in the way she moved, and a primal lustiness in her eyes. The closer it came to the surface, the more it affected him, mind and body.

She was the picture of health. The doctor even said so. Her morning sickness was just a memory. She was literally glowing these days, and her energy level, well, his mind kept conjuring up things he'd like her to do with all that vigor and pep. It just so happened that there were one or two or *a hundred things* he'd like to do in return.

Kimberly switched the burner off and slowly faced her husband. One of the books she'd read said that men were creatures of touch as well as sight and smell. She'd chosen her white sleeveless tunic and soft oversize gold trousers with that in mind. She might have been building her self-confidence, but she still wasn't nervy enough to carry off anything as blatantly sexy as G-strings or garters. Luckily, the expression in Cort's eyes told her he liked what he saw.

Gesturing toward the desk on the far wall, he said, "It looks like you've been busy today."

She nodded, and slowly slid her hands down her bare arms. "If you're referring to the fact that I've set up my computer, then yes, I've been very busy."

He didn't know the half of it.

He removed his hat and strolled closer. Kimberly's experience with men was limited, but there had to be more than stark desire in the dark blue eyes delving hers. Maybe Cort didn't know it yet, but she believed there was love.

As if by unspoken consent, they both stopped, the span of less than two feet between them. She wet her lips and twirled a finger in a fine strand of her hair.

"Ah, Kimberly," he whispered huskily. "You're not making it easy for me to go back to work."

"Then don't."

Her voice was so soft, Cort had to strain to hear. He wished he hadn't told the men he was coming back with the branding irons. When Kimberly reached up and deftly popped open a button on his shirt, he had trouble remembering the men's names.

She was incredible. But he was a man of his word.

Loftiness might have been to blame for the tilt of his head, and good old-fashioned male conceit might have been behind his grin. But *she* was responsible for the desire pounding through him, and for the speed with which he reached for her. He kissed her, once, twice, three times, then turned on his heel.

"Hold that thought, Kim, because I'll be back," he said, reaching for his hat.

Kimberly's mouth very well could have dropped open, but she was too befuddled to care. Mere seconds ago, Cort had kissed her like a man who couldn't be denied. Now he was halfway through the door.

Thinking fast, she swung into action. Opening a nearby cupboard, she grabbed the rope she'd stashed there earlier, then sped to the back door. She reached the little porch before Cort had taken more than a dozen steps toward the barn. Trying to remember everything Tommy had taught her, she let several yards of rope out at her feet and twirled the other end in the air.

With a flick of her wrist the rope went sailing toward Cort. The lasso hovered over his head exactly as she wanted, then slipped neatly over his shoulders. One tug tightened it sufficiently. Another slowly drew him around.

"Not so fast, cowboy."

Her voice held a new huskiness she was proud of, but it was the expression on Cort's face that truly made her want to tip her face up toward the sky and yell, *"Yee-ha!"*

"Kimberly. What in blazes are you doing?"

She inched her hands along the rope's coarse fibers until she reached him. Swallowing, she turned her face into his shoulder, her brief flirtation with shyness. But then her resolve took over, and so did her passion. She raised her face, letting him see exactly what she was made of.

"I'm not going to let you get away this time, Cort."

"I don't think..."

"Don't think," she whispered. "Not tonight. Tonight, I only want you to feel."

"I told Pokey, Mo and Frank that I'd be back."

"Pokey, Mo and Frank are smart, Cort. You've obviously taught them well. Something tells me they'll figure out what to do on their own."

He closed his eyes, but not before she saw the desire smoldering there. She reached up on tiptoe, angling her face toward his. He leaned the tiniest bit toward her. It was all the invitation she needed. She pressed her lips to his and kissed him full on the mouth. And then she took his hand in hers and slowly drew him inside.

Chapter Nine

Fully aware of the tremors of arousal charging through him, Cort faced the wanton creature who was his wife. She was watching him, the rope held loosely in one hand, the glimmer in her eyes holding him spellbound.

The woman he'd taken to bed that first time had been elegant and shy. Now, her hair was pulled up on one side and fastened with a gold comb, her clothing so damned soft looking he could hardly wait to run his hands over every inch of fabric covering her. She was still elegant, but she was also sultry and warm and amazingly brash. He should know. The upper part of his body was still encircled with a lasso of her doing.

He couldn't deny the pulsing knot that had formed in the pit of his stomach, and he sure as hell didn't want to deny the one that had formed lower. Her smile held a challenge he'd never seen before. It just so happened that there was only one thing he liked better than a challenge.

Taking a step closer, he said, "Are you going to remove the rope, Kim? Or were you thinking of leaving me completely defenseless while you have your way with me?"

Kimberly's breath rushed out of her. She could hear the beating of her own heart in her ears, the very air surrounding her throbbing in a rhythm as old as time and as new as the self-confidence filling her mind and spirit.

Taking the last step separating them, she slowly loosened the rope, sliding it up his body, inch by slow inch. "I'll have my way, Cort, but believe me, you won't be defenseless."

A shudder went through Cort. Deep inside him, something seemed to be breaking free, as if all the days of watching Kim from afar, of wanting her and not having her, had built to this fever pitch and could no longer be ignored.

He grabbed the rope and flicked the lasso over his head, dropping it to the floor with a thud. Feeling strong, powerful, he kicked it aside and scooped her up, reveling in the way her arms wound around his neck.

He shouldered his way into the living room and down the short hall. In the past, she'd always allowed him to set the pace. Not this time. She wiggled to get down, rising up on tiptoe the instant he set her on her feet. She whispered a kiss on his chin, beside his mouth, in the hollow of his cheek, molding her body to his in the process.

His hands were at her back in an instant, gliding her zipper down in one smooth motion. With a gentle shrug of her shoulders, her sleeveless tunic slid from her body, pooling at her feet. Her slacks had an elastic waist, and were so easy to remove they should have been outlawed. She'd traded her white cotton underclothes for beige lace. Someday, he'd take the time to truly appreciate them, but now he only wanted them off. Within seconds, they were draped over a chair nearby.

He felt the wild flutter in her fingertips as she boldly unfastened the buttons of his denim shirt. He tried to withstand the brush of her hand as she moved on to his belt, then slowly lowered his zipper, really he did. But his need was too strong to take things slowly, and he ended up kicking out of his own boots and peeling off the remainder of his clothes. Light filtered through the sheer curtains, giving the room a hazy, dreamy quality. They found their way to the bed without looking, landing in the middle of the mattress in a tangle of arms and legs.

Kimberly was so caught up in sensation she could barely think, and it was all because of Cort. His hands were everywhere, his passion matching hers. When his palms covered her belly, she placed her fingers over his and said, "There's nothing you could do to hurt me, Cort. Nothing. Except stop."

"I don't plan to stop, Kim, not for a long, long time."

Yes, she whispered inside her head.

"Yes," she murmured as his mouth covered hers.

Moaning what sounded like her name, he moved over her. For the first time since their first time, he was wild, his need a driving force that spurred him on and on. The room seemed to come alive with sound. It was as if a hundred different drums were being pounded by a hundred different hands. He increased the tempo until she was sure her heart would burst, her breath coming in deep drafts. She wasn't sure how long it went on. She only knew she couldn't control her outcry of delight, and he couldn't control his.

The extent of their passion was nearly as mind-boggling as the outpouring of love she felt for this incredible man. It wasn't until sometime later, after he gathered her close to him, his breathing coming in deep bursts close to her ear, that she began to surface. Closing her eyes, she heaved a deep sigh of contentment, and pressed her lips to his neck.

In her limited experience, sex had been a pleasurable, satisfying act. *This* had surpassed anything she'd ever known, even that first time. This had been wild, uncontrolled, fierce almost. This wasn't sex between two consenting adults. It was so much more. It was a claiming of a man for his woman, a husband for his wife, and vice versa. What had just happened between them was the ultimate gift from one to the other.

It was love. Kimberly just knew it.

She caught her breath. Strangely, the noise inside her head didn't diminish. He raised his head as if he, too, finally realized that there was more to the sounds filling the air than the pounding of his own heart. He rolled to his side and was on his feet in a heartbeat.

"What's wrong?" she asked.

"That's hail." He reached for his jeans and briefs, his gaze coming back to hers. "Hailstones are a rancher's worst nightmare. They can flatten wheat fields, ruin corn and spook cattle into stampeding. I'm sorry, Kimberly. I intended to make this last all night, but I've got to go."

She rolled to a sitting position and slowly stood. Rather than gathering up her clothes, which were scattered from one side of the room to the other, she marched to the closet and took out her pale blue robe. "There's no need for you to be sorry, especially after what just happened between us. Besides, the last I knew, you couldn't control the weather. If you have to go, you have to go. Just promise me you'll be careful."

Her robe was on and was securely tied at her waist before she realized that Cort wasn't moving. He was standing near the door, watching her, the lazily seductive expression on his lean face completely at odds with the balls of ice bouncing off the roof.

"Well? What are you waiting for?" she asked, tipping her head at a cocky angle that matched his.

His grin curled her toes. "All right, I'm going. I'll be careful. And I'll be back. I promise."

She followed him out to the kitchen where he kissed her full on the mouth, then slipped out the door. She watched until he'd disappeared inside one of the buildings. Within minutes, the hailstones were replaced with driving rain. Breathing easier, she leaned against the door, listening to the sound of Cort's Jeep as it roared down the lane.

Evening shadows stretched from one side of the room to the other. She flipped on a light, strolling about the room and on into the next, lost in thought. What had just happened between her and Cort had been incredible, invigorating, amazing. Until now, she'd always compared their lovemaking to their first night together. Now, she had a new unit of measure.

Her wandering footsteps took her to the bedroom. The air in the room appeared as gray as the sky outside. Their pillows were askew, the blankets rumpled, the closet door half-open. The place was a mess, and she couldn't have been happier about it.

She was in the process of scooping up her discarded clothing when it suddenly occurred to her that they still hadn't mentioned the word *love*.

That didn't mean it wasn't pulsing between them, inside them, around them. It may not have been uttered out loud, but it was there. She could feel it.

Elated by her new objectivity and self-confidence, she smoothed the wrinkles from the faded comforter and fluffed their pillows. Her thoughts spun to the future, her mind racing. Suddenly, her happiness filled her with so much exuberance she couldn't contain it. Twirling around, she left the room in search of something to do, some way to corral this incredible energy called love.

Cort closed the shed door and automatically strode toward the house. He didn't even try to dodge the mud puddles dotting the driveway. What was the use? He was already soaked to the skin.

It was after two in the morning. It felt more like four. His shoulders ached; his neck felt stiff, and he was cold and wet. And tired, Lord he was tired. All the work they'd done in the past two weeks had been undone during one five-minute hailstorm. One of the herds had plowed through more than a mile of fences. Now, the cattle would have to be separated all over again before branding could begin. But not tonight.

Tomorrow.

Tonight, he was home.

Even as he told himself Kimberly would undoubtedly be asleep, his pulse quickened. He might have tried to convince himself that his haste had to do with removing his wet clothes. But he'd been drenched before, and his desire to get out of his cold, chafing jeans had never been accompanied with so heavy a need.

The porch light reached out to him as if he were a weary traveler. There was a dim light in the bedroom window, too, sending erotic images to his mind. As he neared the house, he caught a movement on the other side of the big kitchen window. His steps came to an abrupt stop, dampness seeping through his soggy boots.

The ancient light fixture cast a silver square onto the wet grass, but it was the way the light glinted off Kimberly's pale blue robe that caught him between the eyes. He stood in the dark just outside the glow of the porch light and watched her for a time, unbeknownst to her. She was sitting in front of her computer, and even in profile, she was beautiful. Her hair shimmered like spun gold, and her skin looked pale and smooth.

He didn't make a sound or move a muscle, so he didn't know how she could have known he was there. But she turned, her gaze unerringly resting on him through the lit window. Her cheeks took on a pink glow. And then, all shyness forgotten, she smiled.

He strode straight to the rickety back porch as if propelled by an incredible force. He opened the door and stepped into the house just as she twisted around. "Oh, my. I don't even have to ask. It was bad, wasn't it?"

Removing his wet hat, he said, "It wasn't good. But I've seen worse."

"What about the crops?"

"Most of them aren't up yet, so there wasn't much damage. Thank God. I've seen entire fields of corn shredded by hail in less than five minutes."

She was next to him in an instant, helping him peel his soggy denim jacket from his shoulders. "And the cattle?"

"They took down some fences, and they'll have to be separated all over again. But they're safe for now."

"You're wet and cold. I bet you've been dreaming of nothing except a hot shower and a warm bed."

"If that's *all* you think I've been dreaming of, you lose the bet."

She must have realized that the underlying sensuality in his voice had nothing to do with hailstorms or hot showers, at least not those taken alone, because her smile was womanly and smug. There was a sparkle in her eyes he'd never seen before, and an excitement in her features that warmed him despite his wet clothes.

He hung his jacket next to his hat. Turning around again, he noticed all the papers spread over the table and spilling off her desk. "What are these?" he asked, taking one page in his hand.

"They're spread sheets and bar graphs and pie charts. I didn't know what to do with myself after you left, so I started fiddling around on the computer. I remembered seeing some numbers when I organized the files in your desk. So I typed in some facts and figures. One thing sort of led to another, and although I still have a few kinks to work out, I sort of wrote a program for your ranch."

She sort of wrote a program? Cort scanned one page, then another and another. One contained the high, low and average beef prices for every head of cattle they'd sold last year. Several others dealt with the productivity of the farming end of the operation, from the cost of seed and fertilizer to the selling price per bushel and the annual yield. One column even figured in the moisture factor and how it affected the final price.

"How did you do this?"

She shrugged one shoulder. "Like I said, I just fiddled with a few numbers."

He had half a mind to swing her off her feet and chase away the note of shyness that had crept back into her voice. But something stopped him.

He'd always known Kimberly was a genius, but the reality of what she could do staggered him. Her mind soaked up data the way the Sand Hills soaked up rain. He'd only been gone for five hours, hardly any time at all considering what she'd done. She'd poured over files containing information about the herd, the crops, even the men's wages, and she wrote a program tailor-made for the ranch. There were bar graphs and pie graphs and graphs he didn't even recognize.

"Kimberly, this is incredible."

Her eyes literally danced with an inner excitement he was only now coming to recognize. Suddenly, he knew what had caused it. She'd been working in her element, using her God-given talent. He'd never known anyone so thirsty for knowledge. Something about that realization chafed his mind much the way his wet collar was chafing his neck.

He rubbed his bleary eyes, feeling the lateness of the hour in every muscle. He was on the brink of exhaustion, and didn't like the niggling sense of dread that dropped to his stomach like lead.

"You're tired, Cort."

He found himself staring into the bluest eyes he'd ever seen. Kimberly looked sleepy but happy, traces of excitement still lingering in her features. Suddenly, Cort didn't want to try to figure out what had caused his pensive mood. He only wanted to get out of his wet clothes and get into a hot shower.

Desire rolled through him like thunder as he reached out his hand and twined his fingers with hers. "Kim?"

He loved the way her eyelids lowered dreamily, and the way her lips parted on a shallow breath while she waited for him to continue. "I think I'm getting my second wind."

They reached the bathroom in record time. He flicked on the water in the shower, his one and only renovation to the house, and started peeling off his wet clothes.

"Cort, you need your rest."

Standing naked before her, he leaned forward and kissed the hollow at the base of her throat, feeling her nervous swallow. "I need this more. Now, Mrs. Sutherland, if you'd care to join me in the shower, I'll show you what else I need."

She smiled and stepped back, every last hint of shyness draining from her face. Keeping her gaze on his, she reached up, winsome and graceful, and knotted her hair on top of her head. The woman-soft smile she wavered at him felt like a kick in the chest. It sent a wave of apprehension through him. Ignoring it, and the quiet sense of desperation that came with it, he backed into the shower, drawing her in with him.

Water, blessedly hot and soft, rushed over his shoulders, sluicing down his back and chest. Closing his eyes, he pulled Kim tight to his body, his need stronger than it had ever been. His breathing was ragged, and so was hers. Nearly oblivious to the steam rising up all around them, he lifted her off the floor.

"Whoa, cowboy."

The echoes of longing and laughter in her voice forced his eyes open. The glint in her eyes was serene; her lips were full and smiling. Cort had a sudden, driving need to taste the moisture clinging to them. But she tipped her head to one side, and his lips missed their mark.

"Rome wasn't built in a day, you know." she whispered.

"Rome?"

She hummed her answer and stilled his hands. "Now, before we build the Colosseum, I'd like to scrub your back."

He barely recognized the husky, throaty tones in her voice, but he knew that gleam in her eyes very well. God, he loved it when she went all bold and brazen.

Turning his back to her, he braced his hands on the warm tiles and closed his eyes. Steam rose up in curly wisps all around them, water bouncing off tiles, running down bodies already slippery and wet. Kimberly kissed him, and touched him, and took him to the edge of heaven. And she did it all in her own sweet time.

"For crying out loud, boy," Pokey grumbled. "Even Rome wasn't built in a day."

Cort looked up from the fence he was putting back together and scowled at the snickering cowhands. Mo and Frank were setting posts, and he, his father, Will and Pokey were fixing broken boards.

He liked the way Kimberly built Rome a lot better.

"Can't blame the boy for being in a hurry, Pokey," Joe said. "He's anxious to get back to his bride."

Cort, who was the butt of more snickering, didn't bother with a reply. Will caught his gaze, only to cast him a brotherly wink and a helpless shrug on his way by with a piece of lumber.

Last night's storm had dumped more than an inch of rain on the area, thereby rendering the soil too wet to plough or plant. Unfortunately, fences could be mended in any kind of weather.

"That ain't no reason for him to try to work us to death," Pokey grumbled.

Cort glanced up in time to catch his father's wink, and was struck with the similarities to Will. "You've obviously never been a newlywed, Pokey," Joe declared.

"Kimb'rly is a pretty little thing, that's for sure," Pokey answered. "Ain't never seen clothes like hers before. Why, she reminds me of a hothouse flower out here in the middle of a patch of wild clover."

Cort tried to tell himself that the reason he suddenly felt like slamming his shoulder through the board he'd just fastened was because he didn't like anyone talking about his wife as if he weren't there. But he knew there was more to it than that.

What Pokey said was true. Kimberly wasn't like the women around here. And it wasn't just her clothes. He didn't care how she dressed. Hell, as far as he was concerned, she didn't have to wear anything at all. No, it wasn't her clothing that had him feeling like climbing out of his own skin. It was something else, something he couldn't quite put his finger on.

Will, Frank and Mo climbed into the Jeep and drove on up to another section of fence that had been demolished by the herd during last night's storm. Their departure left Cort with his father and Pokey.

"Once knew a little woman down in San Antone," Pokey declared. "Can't recollect her name, but she had the prettiest brown eyes I ever did see. Made the mistake of mentioning marriage. Next thing I knew, she was bustling 'round my place, hangin' curtains and buyin' doodads and whatnots. I told her in no uncertain terms that I ain't the doodad type.''

Scratching his scraggly beard, he peered all around and said, "I wonder whatever happened to her."

Joe made a sound in the back of his throat and said, "She probably married somebody who *appreciated* her. I remember when Evvie and I were first married. She sewed curtains and dust ruffles and God only knows what else. Why, it got so I hardly recognized my own place anymore. Every night when I went inside, she took me from room to room, showing me what she'd done, her smile prettier than a Nebraska sunset."

"Doodads," Pokey groused. "What is it with women and their doodads?"

"I don't know, Pokey," Joe said, staring out over the landscape. "But nobody can make a house a home like a woman can. Isn't that right, son?"

Cort swallowed hard, then turned away, all his attention suddenly trained on the hammer in his hand. He could feel his father's eyes on him, and searched for a plausible explanation for the disturbing alarms going off in his head.

If his father thought it was strange that Cort hadn't answered, he didn't let on. Instead, he said, "Last time I talked to her, Kimberly mentioned that her things have arrived from Boston. Why, I'll bet she's added some fine touches to that old house of yours. One of these days, your mother and I are going to stop in to see them."

The niggling doubt that had been hovering in the back of Cort's mind slowly grew. Now that he thought about it, Kimberly hadn't changed anything in the house. Oh, it was cleaner than it had ever been, but other than an unfamiliar pan or two and a closet full of clothes, everything was exactly as it had been before she arrived. He wasn't sure what that meant, or why it bothered him. But it did.

Hell, he said to himself, driving a nail in with three hard blows of the hammer. This was the nineties, and women didn't spend their days making curtains and baking cookies. There was nothing wrong with that. Nothing at all. Why, then, was the niggling doubt in the back of his mind growing into a dull ache of foreboding?

Everything was going to be fine. Kimberly married him, didn't she? There was absolutely no reason for this sense of dread hovering over his head. None whatsoever.

That sense of dread followed him around like a storm cloud all morning. No amount of sweating or swearing could chase it away. At two in the afternoon, he decided that maybe he should stop by the house and talk to Kimberly just to prove to himself that everything was all right.

She was on the phone when he walked in the back door, but she looked up at him, her smile calling to mind a phrase his father had used earlier. *Prettier than a Nebraska sunset.* For some reason, it didn't make Cort feel any better.

"Certainly, Mr. Ramsey. Bud. I'd be happy to go over your ledgers. Yes, that sounds like a reasonable and fair amount."

A line formed between her eyes as if her conversation suddenly required all her concentration. But nothing could have dulled the sparkle in their depths. Cort was coming to recognize that sparkle. It was the most vivid when her mind was working overtime.

She turned toward him the instant she hung up the phone. Smiling and radiant, she said, "News travels fast out here. Evidently, the word is out that I've been doing some accounting for this ranch. Bud Ramsey is the second rancher to call today asking if my computer services are for hire."

"Are they?" he asked. "For hire, I mean."

She made a face and shrugged good-naturedly. "I enjoy it so much I hardly feel right charging them."

There, see? Cort thought to himself. *Everything's going to be fine. Kimberly's happy. There's absolutely no reason for me to worry.*

Why, then, did he feel as riled as a wet hornet?

His hand came up to knead the bunched muscle in the back of his neck, his gaze falling to an official-looking envelope bearing the logo of a nationally renowned computer company.

"What's that?" he asked, striding closer.

"That? Oh, it's nothing."

His eyes narrowed suspiciously.

"Well, actually," she stammered. "It's a job offer."

"A what?" He stopped walking, the nagging sensation coming back to his mind like the bong of a Chinese gong.

Kimberly placed both hands on the desk and stood. This was the second time she'd glimpsed this quiet desperation in Cort's expression, and the second time it disappeared before her very eyes. Last night, she'd blamed it on fatigue. She wasn't sure what to make of it today.

"Cort, is something wrong?"

There it was again, a look too fleeting to decipher, but too serious to ignore. Holding her ground and his gaze, she said, "Cort, what is it?"

He strode closer. But not too close.

"I guess that depends. Are you going to take the job?"

Suddenly, Kimberly thought she understood what was behind his pensive mood. He was worried she might leave. Resolving to set his mind at ease, she planted her hands on her hips and said, "I think it would be a little too far to commute, don't you?"

A hundred images converged in Cort's mind at once. Kimberly was at the heart of every one. He saw her as she'd been the night she told him about the baby, and how nervous she'd looked walking down the stairs the night they wed. But the most vivid images were those in which she was busy sorting information and figuring out numerical equations in her head.

With the swiftness of a flash of lightning, he knew what the storm cloud hanging over his head was made of. Guilt.

He'd never known anyone so thirsty for knowledge, or so eager to please. Kimberly had brought so much into his life—sunshine, laughter, the promise of a child. His heart ached around the edges at the thought of that child. His child. Their child. But there was more than a baby to consider here. There was the baby's mother. A person with Kimberly's mind deserved to use it to her fullest potential.

He had no idea how she spent her days, but as far as he knew, her things were still boxed up in the spare room. She'd seemed content enough for the most part, but contentment wasn't the same thing as the excitement he'd seen in her eyes when she'd shown him the program she'd written for the ranch. He wondered how long it would be before she grew bored out here in the middle of nowhere. What could he and this ranch offer someone like her?

"Tell me something, Kimberly," he said, gazing out the window. "Do you miss Boston?"

"Do you miss oranges while you're eating apples?"

What the hell kind of answer was that? What did apples and oranges have to do with anything? He ran his hand through his hair, thinking that it was just like a genius to talk in riddles. And yet it drove home the point he'd been trying to dodge all day. He'd always tried to be responsible. He'd always tried to do the right thing. Now he wasn't so sure he'd done either.

Kimberly had no idea what had put the pensive note in Cort's voice, but she wanted to settle things between them once and for all. Striding purposefully to the big kitchen window, she said, "City life has a certain appeal. There are museums and shopping and people. Boston has an incredible sense of history. There's an energy there, like a pulse. It's catching. But do you know what, Cort? Everyone looks at the same sky, the same moon, the same stars, no matter where they are."

"Then you're not sorry I railroaded you into marrying me?"

Kimberly's heart swelled with feeling. This was it. She just knew it. Cort was on the verge of telling her he loved her.

For a long moment, she took a frank look at him. His hair was in need of a trim, his face in need of a shave. He was still the most handsome man she'd ever seen.

Feeling buoyed by her newfound self-confidence, she raised her chin and quietly said, "I'm not sorry, Cort. Now it's your turn. Are you sorry I showed up on your doorstep in April?"

He glanced down at her sharply, the look in his eyes scattering her confidence like dust in the wind.

"What kind of a question is that?"

A shiver of apprehension snaked down her spine. Summoning up all her courage, she said, "An honest one."

His expression changed, and for a moment she thought he might smile. But the moment passed, and a look of discomfort crossed his face.

"Are you sorry?" she whispered.

His gaze fell to an object behind her before coming to rest on her face. "Of course I'm not sorry."

Kimberly breathed a sigh of relief.

"You're carrying my child."

Her breath caught in her throat. Before she could say anything, he crammed his hat back on his head and said, "Now, I guess I'd better get back to work."

She fixed him with a wide-eyed stare he didn't stay long enough to see. He was out the door in four long strides, closing it with a finality that might as well have been a slam.

She bit her lip until it hurt. Unfortunately, the pain didn't diminish the ache in her chest. She'd been so sure that what Cort felt for her was honest-to-goodness love. How could she have been so wrong?

A saying one of her professors used to spout filtered into her mind. *When you hear hoofbeats, don't think zebras.*

Sometimes the most brilliant people didn't have a lick of common sense. She was living proof. She'd heard echoes of desire in Cort's voice. And she'd thought love.

She wasn't a genius. She was a fool. Obviously, good sex had nothing to do with real love. At least not for Cort.

She blinked back the tears in her eyes, but she didn't know what to do about the heavy feeling that filled the place her heart used to be. Taking a deep breath, she tried to tell herself that at least now she knew the truth. Cort cared about her, but he didn't love her.

No wonder they said ignorance was bliss.

Wrapping her arms around her waist, she stared out the window, but she didn't see. She knew she had decisions to make, and facts to face. For the first time in her life, her mind was strangely blank.

After a time, thoughts formed, one by one. Cort had married her because of the baby. It was a good reason. Why did it have to be the only reason?

A dainty fluttering low in her stomach drew her gaze. She pulled the fabric of her shirt tight over her slightly rounded abdomen. Nothing moved on the outside, but inside, the sensation reminded her of how Evelyn's newly hatched chicks had felt cradled softly in both her hands. Her baby had just let her know that he or she was alive and well. It hurt to smile, but the thoughts drifting through her mind hurt even more. She'd felt her child move for the first time today. And today, she'd discovered the real reason—the only reason—that Cort had married her. The fluttering came again just as a tear slowly trailed down her face.

She wasn't sure how long she stood there staring into the blank nothingness on the other side of the window, but when she came to, shadows stretched from one corner of the room to the other. She turned in a half circle, her eyes taking in the old tile floor, the knotty pine cabinets, the metal table and vinyl-covered chairs. Her computer sat on a marred old desk, its cursor flashing like a blip of radar. There were papers strewn about, and one business-size envelope in the center of the table.

Marching to the desk, she flipped the computer off, then swept all the papers into the wastebasket. She grabbed the envelope with the Boston postmark, all set to tear it in two.

Something made her stop.
Smoothing her fingertips over the logo, she opened a desk drawer and carefully placed the letter inside.

Chapter Ten

"Atta boy, partner. If you keep this up, you'll be taking first place in the state fair in another year or two."

"Do you really think so, Uncle Cort?"

"Is the Nebraska sky blue?"

Kimberly smiled, albeit sadly, and walked out the big door on the west end of the barn. Cort and Tommy were on their horses near the corral, a rope in each of their hands. They both wore faded jeans and cowboy hats—Cort's hat was brown, of course, and Tommy's was gray like Will's.

"I think I'm going to be a cowboy like you and Dad when I grow up," Tommy declared.

Cort swiped at the sweat on his brow and said, "Yesterday you said you wanted to be a baseball player, and the week before last you told me you were thinking about becoming a rocket scientist."

"I could be one of those things, I suppose. Or else I could be an astronaut. I wonder if anyone's ever tried to lasso anything on the moon."

There was something about the sound of Cort's chuckle, so vibrant and clear, that sent an ache to Kimberly's heart and made her start to hope all over again. She didn't know whether to raise her face to the sun and laugh out loud, or call herself every kind of fool.

The sun was directly overhead and blistering hot. She considered moving into the shade, but was reluctant to call attention to her presence. So she stayed where she was, watching, unobserved.

It had been almost two months since she'd asked Cort if he was sorry she'd shown up on his doorstep, almost two months since she'd faced the fact that he'd only married her because of the baby. They lived under the same roof and slept in the same bed. They talked about their childhoods, about politics and the weather. And the baby. Especially the baby. It seemed that when it came to their child, they agreed on everything. Although she wasn't due for three months, they'd already chosen a name—Benjamin Joseph, after both their fathers, if it was a boy, and Anne Elizabeth, or Annie, after his sister, if it was a girl.

Yes, when it came to the baby, they could talk about anything—from the proper way to discipline a child, to the importance of immunizations and high self-esteem. When it came to everything else, it seemed as though they'd called an unspoken truce of sorts. He didn't say anything about the names she'd given the new calves, and she no longer expected him to tell her he loved her whenever he reached for her in the night.

Her life really wasn't bad. She spent time with Krista and Tommy, and occasionally she saw Will, Evelyn and Joe. Katrina and Kendra had even flown out for the long Fourth of July weekend earlier that month. Several of the area ranchers had started bringing their ledgers and receipts to her. She enjoyed balancing their books and simplifying their accounting, she truly did. But she hadn't come out here to this long stretch of land near the South Loup River to balance ranchers' books. She came to balance her life. So far, she'd failed.

"Look, Uncle Cort, it's Aunt Kimberly!"

Kimberly shaded her eyes with her hand and was careful to put a smile on her face. "Hi, Tommy. Are you having fun?"

"Yeah. Me and Uncle Cort are practicing our roping. Have you been practicing yours?"

Kimberly's gaze automatically climbed to Cort's. The top half of his face was shaded by his hat, yet she could still make out the intensity in his eyes. She knew he was remembering that night when she'd lassoed him not more than a dozen feet from his own back door. She knew, because she was remembering, too.

Sometimes, when he looked at her this way, his expression thoughtful, his gaze steady, she could almost believe he loved her. But then his eyes would take on a deeper glow, and she'd realize he wanted her. Very much. His wanting always turned into the most amazing thing. But it still wasn't love.

She swallowed the lump in her throat and turned her attention to her nephew. "No, Tommy. I haven't practiced that in a long time."

From the corner of her eye she saw that Cort, too, had turned away. It was all she could do not to cry.

"Well, partner," he said to Tommy. "Do you think you're up to checking on the herd over by the creek with me?"

"You bet I am!"

Cort's gaze lowered, and so did his voice. "We'll be back in an hour or so, Kimberly. Will you be okay?"

Placing one hand in the small of her back, she wavered him a smile and nodded. "I'll be fine. But I want you two to be on the lookout for bulls trying to get into your back pockets."

Cort heard Tommy's giggle, but he was too aware of the tightening sensation deep in his chest to move. He'd used a lot of sayings in his day, but he'd never used that one. As far as he knew, he'd never heard any of the cowhands spout that particular one, either. Kimberly had probably gotten it from one of the many books she carted to and from the library.

Her thirst for knowledge was insatiable. He wondered how long it would be before the local libraries ran out of books she hadn't read.

"Don't worry, Aunt Kimberly. We won't let any bulls toss us over the fence. We'll keep them out of our back pockets, won't we, Uncle Cort?"

Kimberly saw Cort's nod, but she didn't understand why his expression was so thoughtful, remorseful almost. What was he sorry for?

He made a clicking sound with his tongue, and, with a flick of his wrist and a slight jerk of his heels, he turned Rambler toward the lane. She moved into the shade, marveling at the way Tommy mimicked his uncle's movements.

She remembered telling Cort that there was a pulse to life in the city. There was an entirely different pulse to life out here. The country was fierce, the weather unpredictable. It could swing from cool to sweltering overnight. Right now this part of Nebraska was in the middle of a heat wave, and if it didn't rain soon, the drought Joe had been predicting was going to become reality.

She'd learned so much since coming here. Ranching was grueling, fascinating work. She knew what kind of crops grew in Sutherland soil, and what kind of cattle they herded. But there was more to ranching than facts and figures. The men and women out here had a connection, a kind of oneness, with the land. Their calendars didn't follow the same course as those in other parts of the United States. A rancher's year started in the fall, not in January. And summer didn't begin on a precalculated day in June. The seasons were a slow progression of one into the next. They were a feeling as much as a time, brought about by little more than a scent in the air or a change in the breeze.

Yes, western Nebraska was a fierce and beautiful land. But there were other fierce and beautiful places in the world. She distinctly remembered telling herself she wouldn't stay unless Cort grew to love her. Why, then, was she still here?

When in doubt, do nothing.

She never used to spout pearls of wisdom. Now it seemed they were her mainstay.

The truth of the matter was that Kimberly didn't know what to do. She'd never intended to allow things to go on between her and Cort the way they were. She'd certainly never intended to bring an innocent child into a loveless marriage. Only it wasn't a loveless marriage, at least not where *her* heart was concerned.

She heard the deep rumble of Cort's voice in the distance, followed by the ring of Tommy's boyish laughter. Before her very eyes, a pheasant flew across the lane directly in front of Tommy's horse. The flurry of flapping wings and ruffled feathers caused Socks to sidestep nervously. Before Kimberly could do more than gasp, Cort reached over and steadied the smaller horse as if it was the most natural thing in the world.

Kimberly closed her eyes, one hand going to her heart, the other to the swell of her stomach. Cort was wonderful with Tommy. She knew he would be wonderful with their child, too.

But would that be enough?

She'd asked herself that question a thousand times. If she'd expected a simple answer, she'd underestimated the degree of her confusion. What she needed was a sign from above. Better yet, she needed to see the writing on the wall.

She thought about the letter that was still tucked in the desk drawer. She'd received a telephone call from one of the company's vice presidents last week. The man had been extremely gracious and persuasive, offering her more money, an office with a view, paid holidays and flexible hours. She'd thanked him for his offer, and, once again, she'd turned him down. Rather than take no for an answer, he told her to take all the time she needed before giving him her final answer.

What was she waiting for? Christmas?

In the distance, she saw Cort squeeze Tommy's narrow shoulder. Even though she couldn't see the expression on

Tommy's upturned face, she could imagine it all the way from here.

Her heart swelled with feeling. And she knew exactly what she was waiting for. She only hoped she wasn't a complete and utter fool.

Cort swiped his hat from his head and looked around. The grass surrounding his house was brown, the fields pitifully dry. If they were lucky and locusts and hailstorms didn't mutilate what was left of the corn, they might, *might* be able to salvage enough from the crops to feed the herd come winter.

He wiped the sweat from his brow with one shoulder and replaced his hat before reaching into the back of the truck. Being careful not to bump or scratch the surprise he had for Kimberly, he turned toward the house.

He could smell something cooking from here. He didn't know what it was, but he had no doubt that it would be delicious. It wouldn't, however, be beef. His stomach clenched, but not from hunger. It happened every time he gazed at his own windows these days, searching for a glimpse of Kimberly. A knot formed in his throat, untangled and slowly dropped lower.

Kimberly was nearly eight months along. According to her, she was bigger than a barn. In reality, she was the picture of health. She moved slower these days, joking that her center of gravity had shifted. Cort didn't think he'd ever grow tired of watching the way she moved. The heat had been unbearable all summer, and showed no sign of letting up even though it was nearing the end of September. She didn't complain, but he could tell by the way she placed her hand on her lower back that she was growing more uncomfortable every day.

He grasped the bulky object with both hands and levered it close to his chest, reminding himself that Kimberly was nearly due, and as maternal as the virgin mother herself. One good rain shower would cut the dust, cool the air and make this corner of the world bearable. Maybe it would dampen the need that had a way of building deep inside him—the need to connect with Kimberly—the need to make her his all over again.

But it hadn't rained. It was hot, and she was uncomfortable, and he had no business thinking about doing the things he was thinking about doing. Hoisting the object higher in his arms, he reminded himself that he couldn't control the weather, but by God, he could control himself. He hiked one foot onto the first step, scowling at the pull of his jeans.

The phone started to ring before he made it to the door. Setting his heavy bundle on the porch, he strode into the kitchen, grabbing the phone up in the middle of the fourth ring.

"H'lo."

He spoke into the mouthpiece, but looked around for Kimberly.

"Yeah, Whitie, I'm okay. How about you?"

She was nowhere in sight.

"Kimberly is expecting your call, you say? Something's bubbling on the stove so I know she's here somewhere, but I just walked in the door and haven't seen her yet. You want to add what to your ledger?"

Papers fluttered and the stapler rattled as he searched for something to write on. "Hold on a minute, Whitie. Now I need a pencil or pen."

He flipped through a stack of folders on the desk, then pulled open the drawer. He grabbed a thin gold pen and had just finished jotting down the message when footsteps sounded behind him. The glance over his shoulder was automatic, and so was the slowing of his heart.

Kimberly was standing in the doorway, looking for all the world as if she'd just stepped out of the shower. Her hair was long and loose, the wisps framing her face curly and damp. The fan on the floor fluttered her airy dress, the pale yellow color showing off the tanned length of her arms and the smooth column of her throat.

"Did you get that, boy? Boy? Yoo-hoo, are you there?"

It took a moment for Cort to come back to earth and realize that the low drone coming from somewhere in the vicinity of his shoulder was Whitie Brubaker, and not the sound of his own blood chasing through his veins. Lifting the phone back to his ear, he said, "Yeah, Whitie. I'm here. Okay, I've got it. If Kimberly has any questions, I'll have her call you."

He dropped the phone back into its base without looking.

"Was that Whitie Brubaker?" she asked.

He nodded, and she shook her head, saying, "That's the third time he's called today."

"He probably has a crush on you."

She rolled her eyes. "It's so nice to know that an eighty-year-old man who's nearly as blind as a bat wants me."

Cort felt mesmerized by her smile, the light in her eyes stoking the fire that was already burning inside him. His gaze dropped from her face, to her shoulders, to her breasts.

Whitie Brubaker wasn't the only one who wanted her.

The pen slipped out of his hand. Cort glanced down in time to see it bounce off the top of the desk and roll into the drawer. It landed on top of a business-size envelope bearing the logo of the company that had offered Kimberly a position months ago. In Boston.

Everything inside him went very still.

Kimberly strolled a few steps farther into the kitchen. Although his back was to her now, she was sure she'd glimpsed a warm, all-male responsiveness in Cort's expression moments ago. Each time she saw that glimmer in his eyes, the tiny spark of hope deep inside her grew.

Certain that there was still a chance for the two of them to make a life together, she strode to the stove and stirred the clam chowder, saying, "I heard a word on the radio I haven't heard in quite some time."

"What word was that?" he asked.

Was it her imagination, or did his voice sound strained?

"Rain," she answered, wondering at the change in him. "What else did you do today?"

His voice *was* distant. For the life of her, she didn't know why. Hoping to lure him out of his sudden dark mood, she began to talk about the one thing that always drew them together.

"I went into North Platte to do some shopping. Two women stopped me in the baby department. One of them claimed you can tell the sex of a child by the baby's heart rate. The other one said that has nothing to do with it. According to her, it's all in the way I'm carrying the baby. All out front supposedly means it's a boy, and if you look nearly as pregnant from the back as you do from the front, it's a girl."

She stopped stirring, momentarily thoughtful. "Or was it the other way around?"

The mellow sound of Kimberly's voice worked over Cort like cool shade on a hot day. While he soaked up its comforting relief, she laid the spoon down and reached into a sack nearby, bringing out a tiny white article of clothing.

"I bought a dozen of these little sleepers, and boxes and boxes of diapers." Unfolding a disposable diaper, she continued. "Look at this. Have you ever seen anything so tiny? The saleslady assured me it would be huge on the baby at first. I've studied the diagrams in my books, but I've never diapered a baby in my life."

"Not even Tommy?"

She shook her head. "I was afraid he might break. I never even played with dolls when I was small."

Studying her thoughtfully, he said, "What did you do when you were a child?"

"I played board games and read books. And when I was feeling particularly adventurous, I used to sneak down to the park or playground and watch normal kids play."

The fan hummed from the other side of the room, stirring the hem of Kimberly's dress, delineating the curve of one hip and the slender length of her legs. Listening to her, Cort could imagine her as a child, all skinny legs and pale blond hair. She probably never got her knees skinned up like other kids did. Instead of a mischievous grin on her face, her expression would have been serious, wistful.

She didn't deserve the lonely childhood she'd had. But she didn't deserve to be tied down to the lonely life of a rancher's wife, either. Was that why she'd kept the letter from Boston?

"Cort, is everything all right?"

He glanced at her, his gaze falling away to the sleepers and tiny shirts she'd laid out on the counter. Suddenly needing something to do, he pushed away from the cabinet and said, "I brought a surprise for you. I'll be right back."

Kimberly watched him stride to the door, his shoulders squared and rigid, his steps practically burning up the old black-and-white tiles as if he couldn't get away fast enough. She didn't understand him anymore. Not that she ever did. She wanted so desperately to believe that the emotions she'd seen in his eyes a few minutes ago were rooted in love.

She heard a series of clunks and thuds out on the porch. The door opened, and Cort shouldered his way inside, a beautiful old cradle held tight to his chest. He placed it on the floor, running his work-roughened hand over the curved sides.

"My parents used this for Will and me. Isn't it a beauty?"

Suddenly, Kimberly understood the reason for Cort's earlier excitement. He'd wanted to surprise her with this cradle—a cradle for the baby. Everything he did, everything he said, everything he worked for, was for the baby.

An ache started in her chest and slowly rose to her throat. She went through the motions of exclaiming over the intricate carvings on the old wood, but inside, her spirits, her hopes and her dreams slid away.

Kimberly was only vaguely aware of the breeze whistling through the dark house and of the goose bumps dancing up and down her bare arms. In some far corner of her mind, she understood what the change in temperature meant. A cold front was moving in, bringing relief after months of hot weather. A few days ago she would have laughed out loud and spread her arms wide, welcoming, embracing, the soothing breeze. But not tonight. Tonight, she hugged her arms close to her body and wandered from room to room, lost in thought.

Somewhere in the old house, a wall clock ticked, and every now and then floorboards creaked beneath her feet. She had no idea how long she wandered, or how far she walked. All she knew was that it would be useless to try to sleep, just as she knew it was useless to go on pretending everything was going to be all right.

She came out of her daze inside the doorway of the room that was waiting to be transformed into the nursery. Moonbeams slanted through the window, touching upon walls that needed wallpaper, and floors that needed colorful rugs. The mobile she bought was still in the box, the tiny sleepers and soft blankets waiting to be put away. The silver rays of light threw a cradle-shaped shadow on the wall. Studying the curved lines of the shadow, her hands automatically crossed over her heart.

She'd asked for a sign from above, for writing on the wall. Staring at that shadowy pattern, she understood why people said be careful what you wish for.

Cort Sutherland was an exciting man. Even now, he could weaken her knees with just a look, and turn her insides to feather down with the slightest touch. She knew he wasn't perfect. After all, she'd glimpsed his ornery side on more than one occasion. But he was a hardworking, responsible man, a man of honor, *a man of his word.*

Her brow furrowed over that last thought. Yes, Cort was a man of his word. And he'd never uttered one word about love, not in passion, not even in passing. He'd married her because of the baby. It didn't take a genius to figure that out. He'd told her so months ago, practically word for word. And he'd shown her in nearly everything he'd done since.

The baby rolled, shifting from one side of her stomach to the other. She could feel the flutter kick of two tiny feet, and she smiled, love for her unborn child wrapping around her like an invisible blanket. Placing her hand over her swollen abdomen, she knew it was time to face the truth and make a decision once and for all. For the baby's sake. For Cort's sake. And for hers.

Chapter Eleven

Hoofbeats sounded in the distance. Cort shot a cold look over his shoulder and scowled. He was in no mood for company. His father had accused him of being ornerier than a pet snake hours ago. His disposition hadn't improved any, that's for sure.

He hoisted a salt lick from the back of the Jeep just as Pokey pulled his horse to a stop three feet away. With a mouth full of cuss words and a cheek full of chew, the old man sputtered, "A storm's brewin' as sure as hell. Just look at it, sittin' out there, simmering, working itself into a tizzy. Anytime now, it's gonna circle back this way. You just watch."

Cort crammed his hat lower onto his head and eyed the western sky. A cool front had moved over this part of Nebraska sometime during the night. It had pretty much minded its own business as it meandered along toward the west. It would have continued to do so, too, if it hadn't met up with the warm front out there over the Sand Hills. Pokey was right. Holy hell was about to break loose. The wind had already picked up, the clouds whirling together to form a huge gray wall that seemed to be closing in on them from three directions.

"You didn't have to ride all the way out here to tell me that," he bit out. "I know a storm when I see one."

"That ain't why I came out here. I want to know what you did to make Kimb'rly cry."

Cort jerked around. "Kim's crying?"

"She was."

"Why?"

"That's what I'm asking you. Found her crying her eyes out to one of the horses a coupl'a hours ago. Along with her sobbing, I heard her say sumpthin' about doing the right thing and being sorry."

The knowledge that Kim had been crying added another layer to Cort's dark mood. A storm was brewing, and Kim was crying. He couldn't do anything about one and didn't know what to do about the other.

Pokey's Appaloosa whinnied and backed up nervously. Pokey laid a leathery hand on the horse's mane and said, "Whoa, Stomper. Easy, fella." Glancing down through narrowed eyes and bushy white brows, he said, "This storm's gonna be spiteful. You just watch."

Pokey might have blamed the gathering storm for Stomper's skittishness, but Cort knew better than to blame his own foul mood on the weather. His unease had started yesterday when he'd found that letter in Kimberly's desk drawer. And it had grown this morning when she'd had trouble meeting his eyes.

"You gonna tell me what ya did to make Kimb'rly cry?"

"I don't know, all right?" Several of the cattle turned at the harsh sound of Cort's voice.

"I ain't seen a woman yet who wept without a reason. What were ya doing fightin' with her at a time like this?"

"We haven't been fighting."

"Yeah, I've seen the way you *don't* fight with your father."

Cort glanced toward home, his misgivings increasing by the second. Suddenly, he remembered the way Kimberly had looked after he'd shown her the cradle last night, and the way she'd turned, as regal as a queen, and slowly walked away. Two storms were brewing, all right—one out on the range, and one in his own house.

No matter what Pokey thought, he and Kim hadn't argued. They hadn't even raised their voices. Why, then, hadn't her smile reached her eyes since?

Both Will and their father had assured him that women were always more emotional and sensitive when they were pregnant. But Kim had been crying, pouring her heart out to her favorite horse in the middle of the day. The thought knotted his stomach. This was more than hormones. He could feel it just as surely as he could smell rain.

He eyed the Jeep and the broken path curving over the hilly ground, his thoughts as thunderous as the clouds in the distance. "Pokey, I have to go home."

"Now you're talkin'."

"I need your horse."

"Why not take the Jeep?"

Impatience snaked down Cort's spine. "Because it'll be faster to go the way the crow flies."

Pokey climbed down stiffly, his old bones cracking and popping like corn over an open fire. Handing the reins to Cort, he said, "All right, all right. No need to get huffy. Stomper's all yours. You tell that little woman you're sorry, ya hear?"

A cold knot formed in Cort's stomach, followed by an ominous sense of foreboding. Sorry? He was sorry all right, sorry as hell, and he didn't even know what for.

He turned the Appaloosa and set off at a gallop. They moved like the wind, somehow managing to outrun the storm. There didn't seem to be any way to outrun his sense of impending doom.

It wasn't until he rounded the last curve in the lane thirty minutes later that he finally got a clear view of his place. His truck wasn't in the driveway, and the house was shut up tight. Warnings echoed inside his head, setting off alarms that left a bad feeling in the pit of his stomach. Kimberly wasn't back from her doctor's appointment yet. That meant she'd be out there when the storm hit.

He eased off Stomper and led him into the barn, the wind stirring up loose straw and dust along the way. He slid the bridle over the horse's head, unfastened the cinch, then heaved the saddle onto the rack, hating the sense of inadequacy dogging his every move.

Kimberly is fine. There's no reason to worry. She's driven the truck dozens of times. For a city girl, she handles it pretty damn well.

He felt better—for about half a second. And then his misgivings dumped over him like a bucket of ice water all over again.

Cort slammed the telephone down so hard it bounced. That had been the fourth call he'd made, and no one had seen Kimberly since she left the doctor's office more than two hours ago—not his mother, not Krista, not even the librarian in North Platte.

The rain was coming down in gray sheets and showed no signs of letting up. It pelted the windows and washed over the roof in a frenzied deluge, flowing over the hard, packed earth before following the dips and gullies that eventually led to rivers and streams. There were flood warnings for three counties. The roads had to be treacherous, and no windshield wipers in the world could cut through the blinding torrent long enough for a driver to actually see.

He hated doing nothing. Hell, twice he'd put on his coat and hat, intent upon going in search of his wife. But he'd stopped on the small porch because he had no idea where she might be.

He ran his hand over his eyes, past his mouth and on down the stubble of his day-old beard. He'd always prided himself on his ability to do the right thing. It was getting pretty damned difficult to tell what the right thing was.

He'd vowed to take care of Kimberly and make her happy. Any idiot could see she was miserable. He'd promised to keep her safe. She was probably out in the storm right now.

Creeks were rising, their currents strong enough to take trees and stumps and anything unfortunate or unwise enough to be caught in the low areas along its path.

Kimberly was smart. She was a genius, for God's sake. She'd know enough to stay on high ground. He hoped.

His pacing took him to the room he and Kimberly had shared these past five months. Burying his fingers in the folds of the green satin robe hanging on a hook behind the door, he looked around. The bedroom was neat and tidy, the bed made. Except for a pair of earrings that were lying on the dresser, pastel-colored clothes peeking from the closet and books stacked on the nightstand, the room looked very much as it had before Kim came to live here. Why, then, did he feel her presence everywhere?

She wasn't like any other woman he'd ever known. She hadn't been born to ranching. She didn't even eat red meat. She hadn't taken over his house, moving her things in and his things out. She hadn't changed anything, really. Anything except him.

And now he had no idea where she was, if she was safe. He hadn't wanted to let her go to the doctor alone, but she'd insisted. He should have kept her under lock and key, dammit. At least then she'd be safe.

He remembered a conversation he'd had with his father years ago. They'd been watching a baseball game on television and Will was up to bat. It was the bottom of the ninth inning, and the score was tied. Will swung at the first two pitches, then hit a home run on the third. After watching him slide into home, Joe, a man who rarely showed his emotions, had taken a handkerchief from his pocket and dried his eyes.

Cort hadn't thought about that in years, and didn't know why he was remembering it now. He'd always known that his father was the stuff legendary heroes were made of. He'd wanted his only two sons to follow in his footsteps, working the land and bringing in a good harvest. Yet he'd let them follow their own dreams. One time, Cort had asked him why he'd done it.

"Cages make poor homes," Joe had said.

Joe Sutherland was a very wise man.

Cort had tried to follow his father's example, giving Kimberly all the room she'd need so she wouldn't feel caged in, all the freedom she wanted to use her God-given talents. What if she'd decided to use those talents someplace else? Someplace far away.

Like Boston.

He turned on his heel and was in the kitchen in seconds. Yanking the desk drawer open, he ruffled through papers, sending pencils and pens and paperclips flying. The letter from Boston had been in plain view yesterday. Now, it was nowhere in sight. In desperation, he removed the drawer and dumped all its contents onto the top of the desk, putting everything back one item at a time.

The envelope with the Boston postmark was gone.

Cort sank into the chair and closed his eyes. He'd faced the elements his whole life, at the mercy of the weather and the powers that be. He'd been responsible, and he'd been strong, dealing with droughts and flash floods, with loss, and with loneliness. He vividly remembered the day Will left for college, knowing full well that his brother's dream of playing pro-baseball would take him even farther from home. Through it all, Cort had endured.

But this was different. He didn't know how he would endure if Kimberly left for good, or how he would survive if something happened to her.

He strode to the window and looked out at the driving rain. There was nothing he could do except wait. Nothing, except drop to his knees and beg and barter with the powers that be. He closed his eyes and lowered his chin, the floor coming up to meet his knees.

Rain bounced off the top of the truck. The drops were still huge, but they lacked their earlier fury. Kimberly looked behind her, and then in front of her, finally turning the key in the ignition. The engine turned over on the first try. Not that she was surprised. Cort's truck was as trustworthy as he was.

Thoughts of Cort sent an ache through her that started in her chest and ended in a wide pain in her lower back. She'd been parked along the side of the road for more than half an hour, waiting for the storm to pass. She'd turned on the radio from time to time, and with her heart in her throat, she'd listened to reports of flooding. More than one car had been swept into the Platte River. The South Loup wasn't much better. She'd thought she could make it back to the ranch before things got this bad. She would have, too, if the bridge over Crystal Creek hadn't washed out before her very eyes, forcing her to find another way.

She'd heard enough horror stories about what this kind of storm could do to crops and cattle to twist her stomach into a tight knot. *Poor Cort.* Everything he'd worked for was probably ruined.

Maybe she should wait to tell him what she'd decided to do. No, she'd already waited long enough. Eyeing the piece of paper lying on the seat next to her, she took a deep breath and pulled the truck onto the road.

By the time Kimberly pulled onto Schavey Road, the rain was little more than a gray drizzle. A limb was down in the front yard of Cort's house, and the driveway was packed with cars.

She tucked the sheet of legal-size paper into her pocket and threw the lever into park. Her door was yanked open before she could turn the key.

"Thank God you're all right."

Strong arms half lifted, half dragged her from the truck. Standing on the soggy driveway, a light mist falling all around her, she felt her heart turn over at the expression in Cort's eyes. His face had always been shaped by strong lines and masculine hollows, but she'd never seen so much feeling in any one feature. There were lines between his eyes and deep grooves beside his mouth.

"Don't worry, Cort. The baby's fine."

He looked at her as if he was in a trance. "Oh, yeah, the baby. That's good. I mean, I'm glad."

She tamped down the hope that sprang to life inside her and said, "Are all the crops damaged?"

"The crops?"

That spark of hope threatened to break free of her stranglehold as she said, "Yes. The crops. You know, the corn and soybeans and hay you planted last spring."

"I don't know how they've fared. I haven't thought to check."

The shock of discovery hit her full force. Swallowing convulsively, she said, "You haven't?"

He heaved a huge sigh, his eyes taking on the intensity she'd come to associate with Cort Sutherland. "I've been too busy worrying about you."

Hope sprang free within her, and suddenly she was afraid she might cry. Her chin quivered, her lips twitched and a lump formed in her throat. Cort's first thought hadn't been about the baby, or about bottomed-out beef prices or scourges of locusts, droughts or floods. His first thought had been of her. Only her.

"Cort, I'm fine. In fact, I'm more fine than I've ever been in my entire life."

"I thought you left me. Or worse."

Covering the sheet of paper in her pocket with one hand, she placed her other hand on his lean cheek. Later, she'd tell him about the lease for an apartment in North Platte she'd brought home to sign. And then, they'd tear it up together. But first, she wanted to savor the wondrous emotions in his eyes. First, she wanted to savor his love.

"As you can see, I really am fine, Cort. And I'm not about to leave the best thing that's ever happened to me. Not even if you are a man of few words."

She laughed out loud at the way he looked that very second, his shoulders straight, his hips thrust forward, his limbs long and loose jointed like the true cowboy he was. "I'm not a man of few words."

"Then you'll come right out and say you love me?"

A dawning look of realization passed over his features, parting his lips, lowering his chin, darkening his eyes to the color of the sky. "Oh, my God. I love you."

He said it so quietly, she wasn't sure who he was speaking to—her, or himself. But it didn't matter, because he said it, and she could tell by the look in his eyes that he felt it. So much happiness welled up inside her she thought her heart might burst.

He leaned forward and kissed her, his lips strong, coaxing and full of promises he didn't have to say out loud. She kissed him back, willing all the love she felt for him to be conveyed in that simple, exquisite joining.

Cupping her face in his big hands, he deepened the kiss, his breath coming in drafts, a masculine sound floating from the back of his throat. When their lips finally broke apart, he rasped, "I love you, Kim. And I think it's high time we took that honeymoon I promised you. In fact, I'd like it to begin right now."

He turned her into his arms, which wasn't easy these days, then drew her with him toward the house. Partway there, he stopped and groaned out loud.

"Cort, what is it?"

"There's something else I forgot to tell you."

"What?" she asked.

"My parents are here, and so are Will, Krista and Tommy, and Pokey, Mo and Frank."

She glanced at the windows, waving at all the people who were peering out. She started to laugh, only to stop suddenly.

"There's something I have to tell you, as well."

"Don't tell me, Kendra and Katrina are coming, too."

She swallowed, and took a cleansing breath through her mouth. "I haven't called them yet, but I think I should. The baby's coming sooner than we expected."

The rain had stopped completely, the entire world strangely silent, waiting for Cort to speak.

"How soon?"

"Today."

The sun poked through the clouds. Family and friends poured onto the porch, and Cort's voice rang out over them all. "Today? You can't have the baby today!"

"Sure I can. Just watch me."

Kimberly's knowing smile nearly brought Cort to his knees, but the sparkle in her eyes made him feel like strutting. In a voice that was half growl, half whisper, he said, "Now look who's bragging."

She took his hands in hers and placed them both over her hard stomach. Meeting his gaze, she said, "You know what they say. It ain't bragging if you can really do it."

"Aw, hell."

"What?" she asked.

"At this rate, we'll never get that honeymoon I promised you."

"We'll get our honeymoon, Cort. I'm sure of it."

She looked at all the people spilling onto the porch, at all the people who loved her, and who loved Cort, and their child. Raising her face to the sky, she started to laugh.

Her laughter was cut short as a pain started in her back and squeezed forward with a force that rendered her momentarily speechless. "Cort?" she said when the pain ended. "I think we should go to the hospital. Dr. Grady examined me very thoroughly. He said he wouldn't be at all surprised if I went into labor early, but I don't think either of us expected her to be born today."

Cort went momentarily still. "Her?"

She looked up at him and nodded, and his breath caught in his throat. This was Kimberly, his wife, regal even now, strong yet vulnerable, shy, and doing everything in her power not to be.

"It's just a feeling I've been having today," she whispered.

Cort grinned. After all, he knew better than to question her maternal instinct. He'd been thinking of the baby as a boy, but suddenly, he imagined a blond-haired little girl sitting in the saddle in front of him, telling him things he didn't know. After all, any child of his would feel the connection to the land, and any child of Kim's would be as bright as day.

Joy, excitement and happiness started low in his chest, pushing upward and outward until Cort could no longer contain it. He raised his face and let loose a *"Yee-ha!"* that could be heard for miles. And then he swung Kim into his arms and headed for his truck.

Glancing over his shoulder, he called, "Well, don't just stand there everybody. Let's go to the hospital. Kim and I are having a baby."

There was a flurry of activity behind him as everyone began talking at once. Pokey and Mo couldn't find their hats and Tommy wanted to know why he couldn't watch his cousin's birth. Cort settled Kim onto the high seat and kissed her again. Lifting his face from hers, he said, "Are you sure you know what you're getting into with this crowd?"

She smiled a Madonna smile and said, "I've never been more sure of anything in my entire life."

She inhaled the rain-washed scent in the air. "Do you smell that?"

He breathed in and shook his head.

She looked all around her, at the soggy ground and sturdy old house and all the people milling to their cars and trucks. The damage to the crops had been widespread; it would undoubtedly be a long, lean winter. But she and Cort would get through it together, just as they would overcome any other obstacles life threw their way.

Looking at the strong lines in her husband's face, she said, "Today is the first of October. And it smells as if summer is officially over. A rancher's year begins in autumn. That means this is the beginning of a brand-new year."

Cort closed her door, his heart swelling with love, and with pride. He blinked back the moisture in his eyes and strode to the other side of his truck. By the time he opened his own door, he was grinning from ear to ear.

"What?" she asked, eyeing his gleeful expression.

"Oh, I was just thinking that you're an incredible woman, and that you're going to make one helluva rancher's wife."

Kimberly smiled. She couldn't have said it better herself.

* * * * *

The first book in the exciting new
Fortune's Children series is
HIRED HUSBAND
by *New York Times* bestselling writer
Rebecca Brandewyne

Beginning in July 1996
Only from Silhouette Books

Here's an exciting sneak preview....

Minneapolis, Minnesota

As Caroline Fortune wheeled her dark blue Volvo into the underground parking lot of the towering, glass-and-steel structure that housed the global headquarters of Fortune Cosmetics, she glanced anxiously at her gold Piaget wristwatch. An accident on the snowy freeway had caused rush-hour traffic to be a nightmare this morning. As a result, she was running late for her 9:00 a.m. meeting—and if there was one thing her grandmother, Kate Winfield Fortune, simply couldn't abide, it was slack, unprofessional behavior on the job. And lateness was the sign of a sloppy, disorganized schedule.

Involuntarily, Caroline shuddered at the thought of her grandmother's infamous wrath being unleashed upon her. The stern rebuke would be precise, apropos, scathing and delivered with coolly raised, condemnatory eyebrows and in icy tones of haughty grandeur that had in the past reduced many an executive—even the male ones—at Fortune Cosmetics not only to obsequious apologies, but even to tears. Caroline had seen it happen on more than one occasion, although, much to her gratitude and relief, she herself was seldom a target of her grandmother's anger. And she wouldn't be this morning, either, not if she could help it. That would be a disastrous way to start out the new year.

Grabbing her Louis Vuitton totebag and her black leather portfolio from the front passenger seat, Caroline stepped gracefully from the Volvo and slammed the door. The heels of her Maud Frizon pumps clicked briskly on the concrete floor as she hurried toward the bank of elevators that would take her up into the skyscraper owned by her family. As the elevator doors slid open, she rushed down the long, plushly carpeted corridors of one of the hushed upper floors toward the conference room.

By now Caroline had her portfolio open and was leafing through it as she hastened along, reviewing her notes she had prepared for her presentation. So she didn't see Dr. Nicolai Valkov until she literally ran right into him. Like her, he had his head bent over his own portfolio, not watching where he was going. As the two of them collided, both their portfolios and the papers inside went flying. At the unexpected impact, Caroline lost her balance, stumbled, and would have fallen had not Nick's strong, sure hands abruptly shot out, grabbing hold of her and pulling her to him to steady her. She gasped, startled and stricken, as she came up hard against his broad chest, lean hips and corded thighs, her face just inches from his own—as though they were lovers about to kiss.

Caroline had never been so close to Nick Valkov before, and, in that instant, she was acutely aware of him—not just as a fellow employee of Fortune Cosmetics but also as a man. Of how tall and ruggedly handsome he was, dressed in an elegant, pin-striped black suit cut in the European fashion, a crisp white shirt, a foulard tie and a pair of Cole Haan loafers. Of how dark his thick, glossy hair and his deep-set eyes framed by raven-wing brows were—so dark that they were almost black, despite the bright, fluorescent lights that blazed overhead. Of the whiteness of his straight teeth against his bronzed skin as a brazen, mocking grin slowly curved his wide, sensual mouth.

"Actually, I *was* hoping for a sweet roll this morning—but I daresay you would prove even tastier, Ms. Fortune," Nick drawled impertinently, his low, silky voice tinged with a faint accent born of the fact that Russian, not English, was his native language.

At his words, Caroline flushed painfully, embarrassed and annoyed. If there was one person she always attempted to avoid at Fortune Cosmetics, it was Nick Valkov. Following the breakup of the Soviet Union, he had emigrated to the United States, where her grandmother had hired him to direct the company's research and development department. Since that time, Nick had constantly demonstrated marked, traditional, Old World tendencies that had led Caroline to believe he not only had no use for equal rights but also would actually have been more than happy to turn back the clock several centuries where females were concerned. She thought his remark was typical of his attitude toward women: insolent, arrogant and domineering. Really, the man was simply insufferable!

Caroline couldn't imagine what had ever prompted her grandmother to hire him—and at a highly generous salary, too—except that Nick Valkov was considered one of the foremost chemists anywhere on the planet. Deep down inside Caroline knew that no matter how he behaved, Fortune Cosmetics was extremely lucky to have him. Still, that didn't give him the right to manhandle and insult her!

"I assure you that you would find me more bitter than a cup of the strongest black coffee, Dr. Valkov," she insisted, attempting without success to free her trembling body from his steely grip, while he continued to hold her so near that she could feel his heart beating steadily in his chest—and knew he must be equally able to feel the erratic hammering of her own.

"Oh, I'm willing to wager there's more sugar and cream to you than you let on, Ms. Fortune." To her utter mortification and outrage, she felt one of Nick's hands slide insidiously up her back and nape to her luxuriant mass of sable hair, done up in a stylish French twist.

"You know so much about fashion," he murmured, eyeing her assessingly, pointedly ignoring her indignation and efforts to escape from him. "So why do you always wear your hair like this... so tightly wrapped and severe? I've never seen it down. Still, that's the way it needs to be worn, you know... soft, loose, tangled about your face. As it is, your hair fairly cries out for a man to take the pins from it, so he can see how long it is. Does it fall past your shoulders?" He quirked one eyebrow inquisitively, a mocking half smile still twisting his lips, letting her know he was enjoying her obvious discomfiture. "You aren't going to tell me, are you? What a pity. Because my guess is that it does—and I'd like to know if I'm right. And these glasses." He indicated the large, square, tortoiseshell frames perched on her slender, classic nose. "I think you use them to hide behind more than you do to see. I'll bet you don't actually even need them at all."

Caroline felt the blush that had yet to leave her cheeks deepen, its heat seeming to spread throughout her entire quivering body. Damn the man! Why must he be so infuriatingly perceptive?

Because everything that Nick suspected was true.

* * * * *

To read more, don't miss
HIRED HUSBAND
by Rebecca Brandewyne,
Book One in the new
FORTUNE'S CHILDREN series,
beginning this month and available only from
Silhouette Books!

This exciting new cross-line continuity series unites five of your favorite authors as they weave five connected novels about love, marriage—and Daddy's unexpected need for a baby carriage!

Get ready for

THE BABY NOTION by Dixie Browning (SD#1011, 7/96)
Single gal Priscilla Barrington would do anything for a baby—even visit the local sperm bank. Until cowboy Jake Spencer set out to convince her to have a family the natural—and much more exciting—way!

And the romance in New Hope, Texas, continues with:

BABY IN A BASKET
by Helen R. Myers (SR#1169, 8/96)

MARRIED...WITH TWINS!
by Jennifer Mikels (SSE#1054, 9/96)

HOW TO HOOK A HUSBAND (AND A BABY)
by Carolyn Zane (YT#29, 10/96)

DISCOVERED: DADDY
by Marilyn Pappano (IM#746, 11/96)

DADDY KNOWS LAST arrives in July...only from

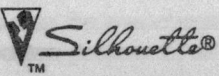

Silhouette®

DKL-D

MILLION DOLLAR SWEEPSTAKES

No purchase necessary. To enter, follow the directions published. For eligibility, entries must be received no later than March 31, 1998. No liability is assumed for printing errors, lost, late, nondelivered or misdirected entries. Odds of winning are determined by the number of eligible entries distributed and received.

Sweepstakes open to residents of the U.S. (except Puerto Rico), Canada and Europe who are 18 years of age or older. All applicable laws and regulations apply. Sweepstakes offer void wherever prohibited by law. This sweepstakes is presented by Torstar Corp., its subsidiaries and affiliates, in conjunction with book, merchandise and/or product offerings. For a copy of the Official Rules (WA residents need not affix return postage), send a self-addressed, stamped envelope to: Million Dollar Sweepstakes Rules, P.O. Box 4469, Blair, NE 68009-4469.

SWP-M96

Who can resist a Texan...or a Calloway?

This September, award-winning author
ANNETTE BROADRICK
returns to Texas, with a brand-new
story about the Calloways...

SONS OF TEXAS

Rogues and Ranchers

CLINT: The brave leader. Used to keeping secrets.

CADE: The Lone Star Stud. Used to having women fall at his feet...

MATT: The family guardian. Used to handling trouble...

They must discover the identity of the mystery woman with Calloway eyes—and uncover a conspiracy that threatens their family....

Look for **SONS OF TEXAS: Rogues and Ranchers** in September 1996!

Only from Silhouette...where passion lives.

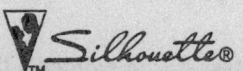

Silhouette®

SONSST

The dynasty begins.

LINDA HOWARD

The Mackenzies

Now available for the first time, Mackenzie's Mountain and Mackenzie's Mission, together in one affordable, trade-size edition. Don't miss out on the two stories that started it all!

Mackenzie's Mountain: Wolf Mackenzie is a loner. All he cares about is his ranch and his son. Labeled a half-breed by the townspeople, he chooses to stay up on his mountain—that is, until the spunky new schoolteacher decides to pay the Mackenzies a visit. And that's when all hell breaks loose.

Mackenzie's Misson: Joe "Breed" Mackenzie is a colonel in the U.S. Air Force. All he cares about is flying. He is the best of the best and determined never to let down his country—even for love. But that was before he met a beautiful civilian engineer, who turns his life upside down.

Available this August, at your favorite retail outlet.

MIRA The brightest star in women's fiction

MLHTM

Waiting for you at the altar this fall...

THE BEST MEN

by
Karen Rose Smith

Marriage is meant to be for these sexy single guys...once they stand up as best men for their best friends.

"Just, 'cause I'm having a hard time raising my three little cowpokes does *not* mean I'm looking for a wife!"
—*Cade Gallagher, the hard-nosed, softhearted*
COWBOY AT THE WEDDING (SR #1171 8/96)

"I swear I didn't know she was pregnant when I left town!"
—*Gavin Bradley, the last to know, but still a*
MOST ELIGIBLE DAD (SR #1174 9/96)

"Why is everyone so shocked that I agreed to marry a total stranger?"
—*Nathan Maxwell, the surprising husband-to-be in*
A GROOM AND A PROMISE (SR #1181 10/96)

Three of the closest friends, the finest fathers—
THE BEST MEN to marry! Coming to you only in

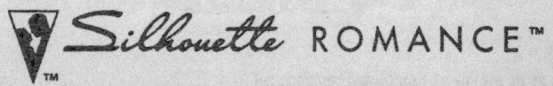

Silhouette ROMANCE™

Look us up on-line at: http://www.romance.net

BESTMEN

FORTUNE'S Children™

New York Times Bestselling Author
REBECCA BRANDEWYNE

Launches a new twelve-book series—FORTUNE'S CHILDREN beginning in July 1996 with Book One

Hired Husband

Caroline Fortune knew her marriage to Nick Valkov was in name only. She would help save the family business, Nick would get a green card, and a paper marriage would suit both of them. Until Caroline could no longer deny the feelings Nick stirred in her and the practical union turned passionate.

MEET THE FORTUNES—a family whose legacy is greater than riches. Because where there's a will...there's a wedding!

Look for Book Two, ***The Millionaire and the Cowgirl***, by Lisa Jackson. Available in August 1996 wherever Silhouette books are sold.

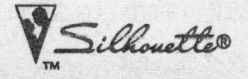

Silhouette®

Look us up on-line at: http://www.romance.net

FC-1

SILHOUETTE... Where Passion Lives

Add these Silhouette favorites to your collection today!
Now you can receive a discount by ordering two or more titles!

SD#05819	WILD MIDNIGHT by Ann Major	$2.99	☐
SD#05878	THE UNFORGIVING BRIDE by Joan Johnston	$2.99 U.S. $3.50 CAN.	☐ ☐
IM#07568	MIRANDA'S VIKING by Maggie Shayne	$3.50	☐
SSE#09896	SWEETBRIAR SUMMIT by Christine Rimmer	$3.50 U.S. $3.99 CAN.	☐ ☐
SSE#09944	A ROSE AND A WEDDING VOW by Andrea Edwards	$3.75 U.S. $4.25 CAN.	☐ ☐
SR#19002	A FATHER'S PROMISE by Helen R. Myers	$2.75	☐

(limited quantities available on certain titles)

TOTAL AMOUNT	$_____
DEDUCT: 10% DISCOUNT FOR 2+ BOOKS	$_____
POSTAGE & HANDLING	$_____
($1.00 for one book, 50¢ for each additional)	
APPLICABLE TAXES**	$_____
TOTAL PAYABLE	$_____
(check or money order—please do not send cash)	

To order, send the completed form with your name, address, zip or postal code, along with a check or money order for the total above, payable to Silhouette Books, to: **In the U.S.:** 3010 Walden Avenue, P.O. Box 9077, Buffalo, NY 14269-9077; **In Canada:** P.O. Box 636, Fort Erie, Ontario, L2A 5X3.

Name:_____

Address:_____ City:_____

State/Prov.:_____ Zip/Postal Code:_____

**New York residents remit applicable sales taxes.
Canadian residents remit applicable GST and provincial taxes.

Silhouette®

You're About to Become a *Privileged Woman*

Reap the rewards of fabulous free gifts and benefits with proofs-of-purchase from Silhouette and Harlequin books

Pages & Privileges™

It's our way of thanking you for buying our books at your favorite retail stores.

PROOF OF PURCHASE
SR-PP155
Offer expires October 31, 1996

Harlequin and Silhouette—
the most privileged readers in the world!

For more information about Harlequin and Silhouette's PAGES & PRIVILEGES program call the Pages & Privileges Benefits Desk: 1-503-794-2499

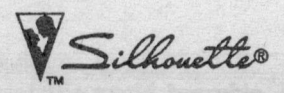

Silhouette®

SR-PP155